MW01139675

TRIANGULATION: DARK SKIES

THE 2019 EDITION OF PARSEC INK'S ANNUAL SPECULATIVE FICTION ANTHOLOGY

Published by Parsec Ink, a subsidiary of Parsec, Inc.

ISBN-10: 1-0820944-3-9
ISBN-13: 978-1-0820944-3-9

Editors: Diane Turnshek & Chloe Nightingale
Assistant Editors: Ana Curtis, Seren Davis, Lara Elena Donnelly, Shannon Eichorn, Katherine Ervin, Emma Flickinger, Kathryn Harlan, Getty Hesse, Kaitlin Jencks, Wenmimareba Kiobah, Nicole Kosar, Emilia Sepúlveda, Malina Suity, Cassidy Teng
Managing Editor: Douglas Gwilym

Cover Art: photo of Pittsburgh from Mount Washington superimposed with the view of the Milky Way from Spruce Knob by Mike Lincoln, more at mikelincolnphoto.com
Additional images from
Atlas Coelestis—London, 1729, John Flamsteed,
Atlas of 25 Celestial Copper-Engraved Charts
Uranographia—Berlin, 1801, Johann Elert Bode
Atlas of 20 Celestial Copper-Engraved Charts
Layout & Cover Design: Douglas Gwilym

Parsec Ink is a subsidiary of Parsec, a non-profit literary organization based in Pittsburgh, PA. For more information, visit our website at: parsec-sff.org.

Parsec Ink
P.O. Box 3681
Pittsburgh, PA 15230-3681

Copyright © 2019 Parsec Ink

All rights reserved. No portion of this book may be copied or reproduced except by permission of the editor, publisher, or individual story copyright owners.

Contents

Introduction

Diane Turnshek

When was the last time you looked up from a dark spot on the earth, free from artificial light, and could see out into the depths of our infinite universe?

Light pollution is a man-made change to our world that has dire consequences. You may know it keeps us from seeing the stars, but are you aware of its harmful effects on plants and animals, or that it also poses risk to human health? Over millions of years, evolution has produced an ecosystem that functions at its best when day is bright and night is dark. We have upset this balance, especially in urban environments.

City planners understand that sustainability and resiliency depend on humans living side-by-side with the rest of nature. They even have a name for it: *biophilia*. What they too often miss is that there's nothing more natural than a dark sky full of stars. Seeing the space that surrounds our planet connects us to our world.

Human beings are the only species who feel the need to announce their presence with booming lightboxes. We regulate excess sound, smell, and physical trespass, but few cities have ordinances about light traveling beyond property lines, invading the windows of people trying to sleep. And the effect isn't limited to the city. Nowhere east of the Mississippi is it truly dark anymore.

Dark sky enthusiasts advocate "lighting smart," meaning lighting only where and when it's needed. Consider the use of shields, timers, dimmers, motion sensors, and lower-wattage and lower-temperature bulbs. LEDs are more efficient and longer lasting than any other light. It's bluer, hotter lights that most interfere with life. Switching to amber-colored, low-temperature LEDs makes a real difference.

Here's something that may surprise you: lighting up the night may make you *feel* safer, but that is an illusion. Statistics show that dark houses are actually less likely to be targeted by robbers, and traffic accidents do not correlate with street lighting levels. If bright "safety" lights kept criminals away, nobody would ever rob a 7-Eleven, right? Does it make sense to spend 2.2 billion dollars a year (in the US alone) to light the undersides of planes and birds?

Light pollution changes the habits of predation, foraging, migration, nesting, and mating of scores of animal populations. Fireflies are endangered, and a billion bird deaths a year are directly related to light pollution. Visit darksky.org, home of the International Dark-Sky Association, to read about this, and much more.

Can you tell I am passionate about these issues? It feels natural to return to Triangulation to help create the edition you hold in your hand, a collection of speculative stories celebrating the night sky and raising awareness of light pollution. On the following pages, you will find thoughtful, mind-expanding, and imaginative interpretations of the theme. We've got to *savor* the stars before we can save them. Will imagining star-filled skies lead to seeing them again? We really hope so.

Enjoy!

Diane Turnshek, July 18, 2019
Founder (and co-editor) of Triangulation

This edition is dedicated to Bear.
"Through Discipline Comes Freedom"

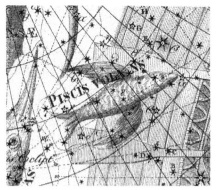

MEIRYTHRO BREVIS

BLAKE JESSOP

The scooter careens through the night. Its solid foam tires kick up rainwater in sluicing arcs that would make little neon rainbows if Hong Kong's streets weren't permanently coated in grit. The rider is swathed in a shiny black raincoat. Bright city lights make her shine like some kind of strange, futuristic beetle. Something much like an umbrella, but spiny and without fabric, is slung across her back. The streets are emptier than usual, and barely anyone takes a second look at her. Shop in Causeway Bay, see weird stuff.

The reason no tourists are midnight shopping is that the night breeze is hazy and foul-smelling. The girl on the scooter wears an insectile helmet with a tinted visor and bulky breathing filters. In the decades since the Handover, air quality has deteriorated so much that Hong Kong is hung with a permanent layer of smog. Wearing masks and finding strange colors when you blow your nose is a normal part of life in the Kowloon Peninsula, but this is worse than anything that's come before. The air is making people sick, and the water in the bay is murky and foul.

The girl on the scooter screeches to a halt in the middle of an intersection and unslings the umbrella. Electric car horns, forlorn street vendors, and a single overworked traffic cop all blare at her. She aims at a bulky grey transformer on a light pole. The thing that isn't quite an umbrella makes a sharp, hard bang, and the girl rocks back on her seat. The street fills with dancing light as the transformer detonates in a sudden blue and gold fireworks display. A colossal thump echoes between the closely packed buildings, and people in slick raincoats flee from the shower of sparks.

The streetlights flicker momentarily, and Fan Mei-li smiles under her helmet. *Stage A complete.* She slings her weapon, hears sirens roaring from deeper in the shopping district, and guns her engine with a high-pitched whine.

The HKPF cruiser screeches to a halt in almost the same place Mei did. A uniformed officer leaps out and starts yelling at gawking passers-by.

"Which way did she go?"

He stops for a moment to clear his throat, then coughs so hard he doubles up and ducks back into the car. His partner cranks the AC, hoping to clear the air. The radio buzzes with ambulance calls. It's only been bad for a few days, and the reports of respiratory paralysis aren't just kids and the elderly anymore. Everyone coughs. The cops dig breathing filters out of the glove box and prepare to go back out.

"Don't bother," the man in the back seat says, "what's the next major intersection?"

"Urmston Road, Agent Cai." The cop is a lot older than the young man behind him, but addresses him with grave respect. He works for the Ministry of State Security. Secret Police or not, Agent Cai blanches.

"Isn't the Castle Peak power station up there?" he asks. Both cops nod. Cai has no idea why a lone-wolf shooter is tearing around downtown Hong Kong shooting up power transformers, but terrorism seems the most likely answer. What kind of person does something like that in the middle of a health crisis? He grits his teeth.

"Well, get moving!" Cai thumps the back of the driver side headrest.

The cops look at each other and buckle their safety belts.

Fan Mei-li designed, stole materials for, and printed the not-umbrella entirely by herself. She did it in less than twenty-four hours, because the air crisis is starting to kill people, and no one is listening to her. She is inordinately pleased with the result; the weapon looks less like a twisted umbrella than some kind of graceful, magic unicorn horn. Mei is much too cool to get caught, but if she did the HKPF would charge her with *possession of a printed gauss weapon* or *terrorism with intent to destroy property,* or more probably both. That would be annoying, because the not-umbrella is actually an air-cored coil gun, not a gauss rifle, and she's in the middle of saving the entire city, whether they want her to or not. She rubs her shoulder under the black raincoat. It probably looks as pale and bruised as the sky. Well, not for long.

She uses her scooter as a shooting rest and aims down the hill at the power station. A huge, blocky set of buildings with tall smokestacks and rack upon rack of industrial transformers. This is the last step.

One by one she picks off the transformers. Each detonation provokes a hail of sparks and a jolt of pain in the meat of her shoulder. The city lights stretching in both directions along the coast go out all at once, and a few seconds later come back on. That means the entire city is on backup power from the mainland. *Stage B complete.* The die is cast, and Fan Mei-li feels a profound sense of relief. She props the not-umbrella against the scooter and stretches so hard the bones in her spine pop. The air has a rotten flavor, even through the filters in her helmet. It's too dark to see the water, but it probably looks gross. Not for long.

It's standing like that, admiring her handiwork, that Agent Cai catches her.

The interrogation room is bright and soulless. A grizzled police inspector questions the girl, and Agent Cai leans against the back wall with his arms crossed. Mei clears her throat.

"What will I be charged with?" she asks with a squeak. She considered getting caught during her planning phase, but the reality of it is only just starting to sink in.

"Possession of a printed gauss weapon and terrorism with intent to destroy property," the inspector says coldly.

A look of extreme annoyance crosses the girl's face, as if she hadn't done any of that.

"I didn't do any of that," she says. Now the inspector looks as annoyed as Mei does. His features narrow the same way a dog's do when it smells meat.

"I got a wife and kids breathing the worst air in Chinese history, and you're running around trying to kill the power."

"Yes," Mei says, and before the inspector can belt her, Cai speaks up from the back of the room.

"Why were you destroying transformers?" the MSS agent asks. Mei cranes to look around the inspector.

"Because you don't have any spares. Hardly any country on earth has spare power transformers. Did you know that?"

Cai didn't, but he doesn't let it show.

"So you didn't make a gauss weapon—"

"It's a *Coil Gun*."

"—and you're not a terrorist."

"No. I'm saving the city."

"The Peninsula is choking on the worst cyanotoxin bloom the Ministry of Environment and Ecology has ever recorded," Cai says. "How are you helping? Who radicalized you?"

Mei looks shocked.

"Cyanotoxins? No, wrong; those are green. How dumb are you? The air is killing people because it's full of a suite of cyclic polyether compounds produced by a previously non-classified dinoflagellate similar, but not identical to, *Karenia Brevis*. This one has some double-bonds that *K. Brevis* doesn't, so it's definitely new strain of bacteria. I checked. It'll need a name, and I want it to be *Meirythro Brevis*. Write that down."

"What are you talking about?" the inspector says. His face backflips between anger and confusion.

"*Erythro* means 'red' in latin, and my name is Mei, so *Meirythro Brevis.*"

No one laughs.

"Come on, that's hilarious."

"You need to take this seriously," Cai says. He can't get a read on the girl. She's either crazy or a genius. He wonders if she can be both.

"I already have. Besides, why should I? You're not."

"I am now," Cai says. Mei believes him. She finally takes a good look at his face. Tired and a little gaunt and more than a little handsome. She starts blushing, looks down, and gets annoyed with herself.

"You should. The HKPF is going to end up looking pretty silly when this is over."

"I will send you away forever," the inspector growls, "and when that's over Agent Cai will send you to the mainland for re-education."

Mei suddenly looks like she might burst into tears. Her face is as easy to read as the flashing billboards of the shopping district.

"No, you don't understand: this isn't about showing you up. It's not about Hong Kong being part of China. Really. That's a different problem. This is about the fact that I knew how to fix the algal bloom and clear the air and no one else did."

The inspector plants both palms in his eyes and rubs with obvious frustration. Cai straightens up.

"You haven't solved anything. The power is still on and the air still stinks."

"Agent Cai," the inspector says, getting up. "I'm going to get some coffee, then I'm coming back to get serious."

The door closes with a distinct click. Silence.

"Do you really work for the secret police?" Mei asks. "Instead of sending me to a re-education camp, you could always claim that I did it on purpose. That's not even a lie. I did do it on purpose. You just didn't know you wanted me to."

Cai just looks at her. Uncrosses and recrosses his arms. The fine wool of his suit rasps under his forearms. He's missing something, and it bothers him.

When the inspector comes back they start all over again, except now he's got the desk lamp tilted so that it shines with extreme brightness in Mei's eyes. He lights a cigarette, and the girl waves her hand at the wisps of smoke.

"Seriously?" Mei says, "Why would I answer you faster with light in my eyes? I'm not even lying to you. Fine, you know what? That's why I'm doing this. That light. It's so annoying you have no idea. You have no idea what you're doing."

"You will find I do," the inspector spits.

"When I save this city and make you look foolish, you will find you don't."

Cai's stomach takes a little lurch downward. That's what he's missing. She's talking about turning the lights out as if she's already done it.

"Why are you talking like you've already won?" Cai says.

"Because I have." Mei shrugs.

"How?"

"This isn't just a red tide, no matter what the Ministry of Environment and Ecology says. You can't just wait for it to go away. It won't. It's going to sit in the water around Hong Kong and choke it to death unless you kill it. Or, more accurately, until someone who isn't an idiot kills it for you."

"And you think you know how."

"I've already done it. Or I will, as soon as the lights go out. Night in this city is a thousand times as bright as a natural dark sky. The problem isn't the bacteria, it's the zooplankton that eats it. Plankton use the diurnal cycle to figure out when to come up to the surface and eat. It's so bright on the Kowloon Peninsula that they aren't surfacing. They think it's daylight all the time, and the fancy, unclassified bacteria in this algal bloom are exploiting the niche."

"But you didn't turn the lights out. You shot up a bunch of transformers with an illegal 3D-printed coil gun."

"That's technically true," Mei admits, "which is my favorite kind of true. Hong Kong uses overhead power lines, and almost all the electricity comes from coal, gas, and diesel, which is gross. That's a problem, but not the one I was dealing with. I blew up transformers in a radial pattern that will put maximum stress on the grid. When I shot up the power station the whole city switched to backup power from the mainland. The point is that all we need to do to kill the bloom is leave the lights off for a few nights so that the Zooplankton comes up and eats it."

"Goddamn it," the inspector yells, "you didn't turn the lights out!"

"Sure I did," Mei says, "or I will, as soon as the bomb I planted on the undersea connection to the China Southern power grid goes off. That'll take a few days to fix, and there are no backup transformers. Problem solved."

The cigarette drops out of the inspector's mouth, and little embers leap from the tip when it hits the table.

"When will it go off?" Cai says, almost choking.

Mei looks up at the wall clock.

"You probably should have asked about that first," she says.

The lights suddenly go out and Mei, along with everything else, disappears. *Stage C complete.*

There's a lot of crashing about in the HKPF building, and people bump into each other in a frantic tattoo. No one really knows how to work in the dark. Mei does. She's been practicing.

A floor map of the HKPF building flashes in her mind. It wasn't supposed to come to this, but she did make a plan for it. She has no idea how she'll survive as a fugitive, but that's tomorrow's problem. Maybe get a haircut.

Giddy with something that's fear or rapture or anticipation, she gets into the emergency stairwell and climbs. The building has weak, battery-powered emergency lights. The hospitals and military will have lights too, but that's okay. They actually need those, so Mei didn't bother coming up with a way to turn them off.

Mei huffs and puffs her way up the stairs, hearing the distant clatter as everyone else retreats to street level. *Be unpredictable.* If she gets away, she gets away. If not, she gets to look at the sky.

The air up on roof resonates with windy treble and howling sirens. The city below is dark, lit only by the ethereal twinkling of cell phone lights as people deal with the power outage. That's okay too. It's not nearly enough to light the sky. She identifies the fire escape and how to climb over the air vents to it.

Before she can execute *Stage E,* she glances up and stops. It ought to be *Stage D,* of course, but she likes *Stage E* better. *E* for *escape.* The reason she stops is the sky, full of stars. It's the first time she's ever seen it. Even with a bit of haze, the crystal glitter of a thousand galaxies is like nothing she's ever seen. It pulls her soul into the heavens, and she forgets about the algal bloom. Realizes she'd have blown everything up just to see this.

That's how Cai finds her, just staring at the sky. He reaches for the gun on his belt and stops, because he sees what she's looking at, and he looks at it too.

"This is going to work," the girl says, "just give it time."

Cai decides to give it time. The dark night passes, and they look at the stars. Mei lies down and meshes her fingers behind her head. The MSS agent strolls the rooftop and watches Hong Kong deal with the dark. There are some fender benders, sirens, and a lot of people on rooftops looking at the stars. An enterprising dumpling stall fires up a propane grill and without the traffic noise, Cai can hear the clash of pans. The wind ruffles his suit jacket.

When an amber glow shows on the horizon above the bay, Mei taps him on the shoulder.

"Have you decided what you're going to do with me?" Her words are clear, a little nervous. Something about them seems off, like they're a digital recording instead of a natural human voice. Too distinct. He turns to look at her, and she smiles. Her teeth are even and white.

"Your mask," Cai says with a start.

"I took it off two hours ago. Try it."

He does. The air isn't clear: it still has the musty smell of living water, but it doesn't make him cough. He realizes he hasn't rubbed his eyes in hours.

"You were right," Cai says.

"You're surprised?"

Of course Mei was right. She knows he knows she was right. Now the only question is what he's going to do about it. Mei-li makes her peace. The show will go on without her, but she wants to see it. She wants to see it so, so badly.

"The fire escape ladders are over there," Cai says. "Keep to the right when you get to Tonochi road or you'll run straight into sentry box at the front door."

"You're letting me go?" Mei can barely believe it. This is China, not Hollywood.

"No, I'm making you an offer," Cai says, and extends an embossed business card. It trembles in the dawn breeze off the water.

"Huh," Mei says. "That's not what I expected. I'll think about it. Can you make sure they name the new species after me?"

"I'll think about it," Cai replies.

Fan Mei-li smiles and plucks the card from his fingers.

"Be a hero. Make sure the lights stay off all night for another two or three days, and the bloom will clear entirely."

Agent Cai nods, and Mei runs, the sounds of both her sneakers and her laughter slapping against the metal safety stairs.

Blake Jessop is a Canadian author of science fiction, fantasy, and horror stories with a master's degree in creative writing from the University of Adelaide. You can read more of his speculative fiction in "I Didn't Break the Lamp: Historical Accounts of Imaginary Acquaintances" from DefCon One, or follow him on Twitter @everydayjisei.

THE SECOND STAR IS MISSING

KATE RUEGGER

I met him once, you know. It was back when I'd mark time in a pub between shifts and sleep, down in the part of town that used to be fashionable but was rubbing its veneer of established fortune thin.

He was beanpole skinny. Adolescence finally catching up, I guess. His hair was tousled, one step short of wild. He sat so still, amid the other patrons' raucous singing and rambling loud whispers, that I could almost see the long exposure photograph, almost feel the way time clawed at his skin as it passed. Dragging him along as he stood, silent, against the tide.

Only his eyes moved. Dark as the night he flew through. Watching for his crew.

I left my empty glass at the bar, paid, and moved closer. Like anyone else, I'd heard the stories. More importantly, heard the whispers that there was something more than talk to him. That he, having escaped gravity and time, knew freedom better than anyone else.

Leaning against his window table, I looked out toward the street, not ready to address him face to face. "I've always wondered..." I began.

He turned to me and cocked his head, that child's instant curiosity in a teenager's form.

"How do you choose your lost boys?"

He laughed, and the low pitch caught me off guard as much as the cynical tone. "You know you're too old, right?"

"Of course."

"You aren't begging anyone's case, then? No sons or nephews or neighbors?"

"No."

He turned back to the view of the street. "These days I'm not sure which I like less: the pleas or the questions."

Taking one last look at him, autumn-red coat buttoned, scarf fraying, fingers fidgeting with an antique bracelet, I stepped back.

"No," he said, shaking his head. "No, walk with me. It'll pass the time."

He stood and led the way circuitously through the crowd to the door. People made way without looking, continuing to text or drink or dance as the young man half-walked, half-leaped around them. I followed, getting bumped into and shouted over in his wake.

We emerged into the street, finally. Cars blew past, churning slush as they went. He forged on, ducking into alleys and crossing streets with an instinct for geography and the gaps in traffic. A few minutes later, we emerged into an older part of town, one with narrower streets and less activity. With the muffling of the snow, it was quiet enough that, after a few minutes of silence, I noticed the hum of the city: the underground rails, cries from children and parents indoors, distance-softened traffic noises.

He finally slowed down enough for me to walk beside him. Not wanting to start off on the same wrong foot, at least, I followed up on his earlier comment: "What are you waiting for?"

"The trains."

"Oh, yes, the snow delays," I replied instinctively, remembering flashes of news alerts earlier today. Then I processed the statement. "You don't—you don't get to, I mean, you go by train?"

His laugh was brighter this time. "No, no. That's one thing they got right. How do they put it? Second star to the right, yes?"

"Yes."

"Look up. Can you see it?"

I followed his direction, looking up into the night sky. The snow clouds had cleared, but with all the city lights, only the moon was visible. How long had the stars been hidden? Why hadn't I noticed sooner?

He must have observed my confusion, because he laughed again, almost bitingly, at his own joke. "I have to take the train outside of the city to find enough darkness to navigate by these days. I spend three times longer here than I used to, waiting for trains and riding on them. Thus," he gestured to himself, indicating his height. "My warranty is running out."

We walked on in silence for a while, moving through time more than space. I let the silence go on.

"You asked how I choose," he said at last. "Most of it is timing. Whoever I find first on a given trip that needs me, who has no other hope. I used to walk the wards of children's hospitals, before security got tighter. These days I watch the streets, the back alleys, the roofs, the bridges. I let 'Darlings' stay where they are."

"Ah," I said, unsure how else to respond as new images slid over old.

"I myself was taken by my predecessor from the barracks of a cotton mill, sick, beaten, and starving. He was in charge for... we aren't very good at dates, so I'm not sure. A long time. A few centuries. And then he was gone. Came back once, to get some things. Proof, I'm sure. You're always asking for proof of where we come from, what you want us to leave behind." He almost spat the words. "When he left us, we had to decide what to do on our own. Two dozen of us, not one looking a day past ten years old, having known each other for decades, just trying to figure out what to do."

He paused, kicked a snow drift.

"Took us a while. But enough of us knew enough pieces of the world to know he had been doing something good. Something we couldn't just stop doing. So..."

He stopped by a streetlamp, standing with his back to me, and rested his pale fingers against it. I saw his shoulders rise and fall in a steady sigh under his coat. Then he went up on his toes and kept going, up, up, coat and scarf trailing lightly, rising with the same soft speed of that morning's silent snowflakes. As he spiraled, his face came into view, eyes closed, the slightest grin of fierce pride on his lips. Then his fingertips began to brush the lantern, and his eyes opened to the bright, reflected whiteness of the city lights on snow. He fell to the ground with a slight stumble.

I went to take his arm, but he moved away, onward into the night.

"Can't fly unless I believe it's dark—these days that means I can't fly in the city with my eyes open."

"The trains..." I said, finally understanding.

"Thus the trains, indeed. The fairies built in the failsafe against flying in the light back when it made sense, before you made night just as dangerous as the day. Of course, they didn't know better—the fairies, that is. I'm still not sure what *they* are. I used to believe they were just little tricksters with strange powers and rules, like in all the stories. I certainly don't believe that now, not after talking to them. But I can't tell you what they actually are either. They could be aliens, at the other end of our... what is it called? A wormhole. Or some of your new computers, artificial intelligence imprisoned on our little island for the greater good." His humor was dry, stale, read off the inside cover of a book at a garage sale. "They're the ones who taught me to fly, taught everyone who came before me. They're probably the ones stopping time. They're the real power on that island."

"You volunteered, though. To take his place when he left," I said.

He stopped again, kneeling by a snow drift. He scooped up a handful of snow, began to shape it with those clever fingers. "There were a limited number of us who could. Some would have died upon re-entry into time, their sicknesses churning back into motion. A few were still too new, had people waiting for them, and others had been away too long, would have been lost in the cities. And... I couldn't let you win."

"Win?" It was getting hard to tell how personal that "you" was.

"Yes, win. In your game of selflessness and selfishness. Do you know how many children I have to walk by, just here in this one city? How many hundreds of millions I have the luxury of rejecting from afar? I—" he smashed the snow figure he had been working on and stood to face me. "There's only so much room on my island, so much food, and I can't bring everyone I find unless I want to run the place into the ocean. Only a few can go home every year, so only a few can replace them. I spend more time helping children find the good social workers, the safe houses, the shelters, than actually bringing them back. Too much time just holding their hands while they..." His hands covered his face, a dark mockery of childhood games. "So many of them don't need to live there, wouldn't need it, if you could just—"

"It's not me!" The words slipped out, finally. Even before I saw the supernova in his eyes, I wished I could reel them back out of the cold winter air.

"It's. Not. You," he said. His bared teeth were like an arm of the Milky Way, slamming down, down, towards Earth, towards me. "How many. How many have *you* walked past? How many, do tell, have you saved? Give me a number. I may not be on speaking terms with time, but I've learned my arithmetic after all these years."

He came closer, hands shaking. I backed into the wall of the nearest building, afraid of that ancient darkness he carried with him in this electrified city.

"I've had to learn it over and over again, study it in their blood and their sweat and their tears as I go on. In the medicine their parents couldn't afford. In the bruises from belts, in the scars from knives in their own hands, in the hollow of their unfed stomachs. They could be here, living in reality just as well and far more happily than they do in the soap bubble of a life that I can offer them, but you refuse. You keep your children locked up behind gates, give them treats and toys while the others beg for scraps, pray for one night without pain, wish for just a breath of freedom. I hear every word, so loud that it's hard to hear anything else most days. And now I'm trapped here, losing hours every night because you're so afraid of the dark that your nightlights have eaten the stars whole."

He paused for breath, breathing raggedly. His hand went to his chest, tugged something out from under his scarf, over his head. A necklace, dark and matte in the light of the streetlamps. Its pendant hovered, unaffected by the light or gravity, rising and falling serenely on the breeze. Like fairy dust.

"It *is* you. Your choices not to fight back. But I'm—" Without his stooping or acting, his years caught on Earth became apparent, the lines taking root around his eyes, the echo of the pain of lost baby teeth, the taut-wire quality of his muscles, no longer soft with infancy. He wasn't old yet, but the weight of the knowledge that he would be was more than enough to compensate for his escape from gravity.

His eyes caught mine and I saw, in his imagination, not a colorful island or romping children, but an old man's corpse, fallen from the sky, unmourned except by those he could no longer protect.

"I am tired tonight. A chance for you." He held out his hand. Offered me the necklace.

I reached out slowly, wanting to feel the smoothness, the paradox of metal lighter than air, that word which points towards freedom in so many languages. I wanted to fly with everything that remained of my child's heart.

"Would you take it?" The necklace shuddered in his hands, smooth silver chain sliding against the floating pendant. I recognized its shape, finally: an acorn, green as spring, dark as tilled earth, small and delicate, but hard against the mortal air. "Would you take my place?" The quiet desperation in those eyes was as menacing as a storm at sea observed from the sunny coast.

We stood, framed in the light that held him here, on this world, under this sky we never looked up at anymore, among so many young people who did. Ones he could not help, and ones I hadn't even tried to. My feathers fell, wax-coated, around me. I let my hand drop.

He stared at me another moment, then ducked into the necklace, tucking it back under his tattered scarf. "All children, except one, know better than to fly. It's my error to make. Find your own." Just a hint of that old childishness mixed with the resignation draped about him.

My phone buzzed in my pocket. I took it out to see an alert from the National Rail.

"The trains are clear!" I said, scrolling through the notification. "They'll be running again in an hour. When will you—"

By the time I looked up, only a slight mark in the snow remained.

Soon he'd be waiting for his second star to emerge from the countryside sky. Waiting for it to find him and a new lost boy again.

I, however, was finished with waiting. Which is why you're here now, safe with us.

Look at the clock, you've gotten quite a few stories out of me! I think it's time you and I both got back to sleep, don't you? You don't want to miss breakfast with the other boys.

Now, off you go. Good night, child. Sweet dreams.

Kate Ruegger was born in Atlanta, Georgia, and grew up in Pittsburgh, Pennsylvania. She reads everything from Austen to Asimov and is also interested in history, cooking, cryptography, dinosaurs, and playing the oboe. A sophomore student of architecture at Penn State, she is a 2018 graduate of Alpha, the Science-Fiction, Fantasy, and Horror Workshop for Young Writers. Follow her on Twitter @kate_ruegger.

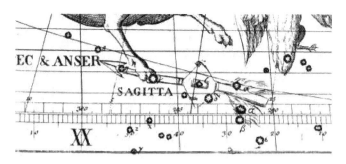

HOW TO GLIMPSE THE ICARUS STAR

MARY SOON LEE

How To Glimpse The Icarus Star

Cast Hubble high into the sky.
Peer through his mirrored eye.

Let gravity augment his sight,
massed galaxies lensing light.

Across nine billion years of night
the image of a star takes flight.

A star, a single blue-hot star,
from almost unimaginably far.

Nicknamed Icarus for a boy
whose fame outlived his joy.

Hubble's portrait so very old,
the star itself long dead and cold.

How to Glimpse the Icarus Star

How To Mislay Constellations

Set them down carefully,
each star in its place,

artfully arrayed against
a bare black backdrop.

Undertake a brief study
of a mere million years:

an initial investigation
of Saturn's interior,

or a preliminary assessment
of Mercury's mood swings.

After writing up the results,
survey the celestial sphere—

your constellations in pieces,
images mangled and reframed,

the miscreant stars skating
the dark sky to new friends.

How To Notice A Dark Nebula

Disregard the galaxy's glare,
the cocky constellations.

Search for a smudged dimness
dusking the brighter sights.

That dirty interstellar dust
disguises secret treasure.

Within her curtained darkness
the birthing stars lie swaddled.

Stay as still as you can.
Do not interrupt her lullaby.

How to Glimpse the Icarus Star

How To Go Eighth

Let the other planets
yield their lesser secrets:

Earth succumbing first,
easy prey to explorers.

Venus the second victim,
viewed by Venera, Mariner.

Mars, Jupiter, Mercury,
Saturn scarcely resisting.

Uranus, more reluctant,
holding out for longer.

When they come for you,
dissemble, play dumb.

Pretend Pluto's a planet,
suggest they visit him.

Anything to distract them
from your own dark truths.

How To Go Seventeenth

Follow your brother to the frontier,
a pair of explorers, Jupiter-bound.

Rush through scorching radiation belts—
a hundred thousand miles an hour—

skimming close to cloud crests,
snapping pictures of the Red Spot.

Fly by, Jupiter's force flinging you
across the solar system to Saturn—

first to ever reach those rings,
up close, braving their passage,

measuring Saturn's magnetosphere,
taking Titan's wintry temperature.

Don't stop. Don't doubt destiny.
Keep heading onward and outward.

(Note: Pioneer 11 was the seventeenth space probe of the Pioneer program.)

Mary Soon Lee was born and raised in London but now lives in Pittsburgh. She writes both fiction and poetry, and has won the Rhysling Award and the Elgin Award. Her book Elemental Haiku, containing haiku for each element of the periodic table, is forthcoming from Ten Speed Press in October 2019. She has an antiquated website at http:// www.marysoonlee.com and tweets at @MarySoonLee.

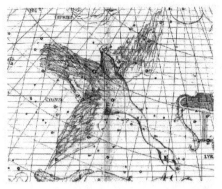

Why We Endured the Darkness

Maddy Dietz

When my back was to the mottled quilt of a spacecraft we'd pieced together, when I was waiting for nothing more than my own small chance at death and beyond, I didn't realize how hard I was praying. I was praying to the stars, to the very idea of stars in the sky, until Harper slid her hand over mine and everything went blissfully blank.

"Hey. Stop thinking so much, Ness," she said. Harper was good at making everything sound brusque and simple and accessible. Angels almighty, you should hear her talk about trajectory and fuel supply like it was simplicity itself. That was how Harper molded the world around her; she ironed life smooth, snipping off any excess until she was left with a clean circle of connected points. All effortless, dotted lines. Like the prayer circles we kept tacked up on the walls. Pretty little halos pinpricked with the promise of light to remind us of what we were hopefully striving for.

"I'm okay," I claimed. "Just nervous. You know, about the potential for horrific death if this thing breaks." Harper had taken my left hand hostage to squeeze it gently, so I smoothed over the hull of our ship with my other, double-checking that no soft sand from the surf still needed to be brushed off. Our project of decades was complete. All that was left was to wait for it to be fueled up enough to make the pilgrimage.

"That's not what you're nervous about." Harper's voice always went soft around the edges when she spoke of this. Her thumb kept catching on the knobs of my knuckles, pushing and pulling the wrinkles on the back of my hand like tides.

"Oh, I'm not scared of dying anymore? All fear is purged from my frail bones? I knew the day would come when I accepted it all. Thanks for telling me."

"I'm serious, you don't have to be scared. No matter what we find, Ness, nothing changes. Status quo remains. If we get out there and find an angel or two, that's icing on the cake." She liked invoking these cutesy olden phrases of hers, things that her mother might have said. But this overarching concept of knowledge and the unknown was a long-ingrained argument of ours, worn to a shine of passivity over the years, so I felt I was obliged to reply.

"Knowledge directly challenges the status quo." Harper scoffed and I smiled; we followed our routine. All the better to soothe one another as we waited. The ship we'd created was beautiful in that it was ours, but the equipment was barely second-rate. Every step had to be taken with the utmost care if we wanted to make it through re-entry.

We'd fired a prototype, years ago, to see what we were up against. The whole thing had imploded before it could reach orbit, becoming its own little star, its own Sun to rival our nearby God in the sky, the only one of the angels we had ever seen. I had felt status quo shift into something doomed and barely-hopeful in reaction to that knowledge. So I stuck to my argument.

"That's false, love. Think of Schrödinger." Harper ushered me over to sit by the dock. Meters and meters removed from the hand-sewn ship we'd made and the mess of computers we'd hauled to the shore. We had to land in the water, after all; we'd packed an inflatable raft and a whole mess of lifejackets and everything. What we'd built would be lost to the sea, but for the knowledge? I was more than willing to sacrifice our ship. As long as we didn't burn up in the atmosphere or drown a few crucial miles out from shore or shatter to bits in shallow water. Too many of those who'd gone before us had failed for me to be able to ignore those possibilities.

I was turning over those same fears in my head, but Harper's fingertips were at my jaw, pulling me back to her. "Schrödinger," she coaxed, "Proved that you cannot use that Copenhagen Interpretation of yours on anything bigger than atoms. No quantum theory allowed, baby. The cat is either alive or dead and knowledge does not and cannot change that. Either the prayers are right, the star charts are right, there are great balls of fire floating through the dark, or there's nothing but vacuum up there. Knowledge won't change that, either."

I laughed, so of course Harper poked at a dimple. "Then why'd you spend half your life being the mathematician to my engineer? Nothing quantum about it, we both know knowledge changes status quo for the observer. You want to know about the angels of the universe as much as I do, love. Don't act so tough."

She grinned, so of course I smoothed my thumb over the deepened wrinkles by the corners of her eyes. "Yeah, you know me. Real tough."

A wind swept up from the sea. It was only a breeze, but it was enough for Harper to turn and scan the sky for any hint of a storm brewing. The sky was a pristine sheet, only just starting to burn bright orange with the setting sun. Harper continued, "I want to be able to prepare myself. I want to know exactly how many more years I have with you."

"Harper," I said, because I was near-certain I would cry on this trip. I didn't want to start tearing up before it had even begun.

"I'm happy with however long we get, sweet-Ness. That's the point of all this. The rest of a human life with you? Perfect. More than I could've ever asked for. We get a star's lifetime too? Then I'll treasure it just as much. But either way, I get more time."

"Look, even if Schrödinger was intending to prove you couldn't view larger concepts as something that nebulous, the experiment still stands true. Dunno whether or not we've got an afterlife in store for us until we get up there, Harper. Don't even know if we'll get much more time at all. I mean, whether or not we land safe and sound is…"

"Completely under our control. We checked every last calculation in fifty different ways."

But Harper was still squinting out at the horizon. We both knew how much risk we were heaping onto our shoulders. Every last person who'd attempted to find a few angels had, no doubt. They'd burned up anyway. Considering how much money we'd sunk into the building process, in the days off work to plan and plot together, it almost felt like we should've bitten our tongues and sold an arm and a leg to get on one of the official Church buses up to space, crammed in like sardines as we waited to see what was left for us after this life by signing fifty different agreements to speak nothing of what we saw on pain of death. For all of our broken-in arguments, Harper and I could fully agree on this point: religion should not be put behind a paywall. We would seek out angels of our own accord.

Our gorgeous, haphazard ship beeped once to let us know the fueling was complete. I helped Harper drag the computers and cords back across the shore in silence, as far away as we could get them. Hopefully they would be out of the radius of takeoff.

All that was left was to strap ourselves in and make good use of all the prayers I'd made. Harper helped me up into the ship, her hand trembling against mine.

"You know what?" I said as I pulled the hatch shut behind us, squeezed into one of the twin seats we'd made. They were overly cautious in terms of support, probably. I hadn't known if we'd be taking off at age thirty or one hundred and ten, so I'd wanted to avoid every last danger I could for the two of us. Now I had one less thing to worry about.

"What? Gonna file for divorce?" Harper teased. She leaned over to buckle me in before herself.

"And try my hand at dating again? Never. I just… realized something." I let my hands feel over the edges of our ship as I spoke, checking every last seam and panel. "You've got Schrödinger right. I've got human nature right. We both win." Harper paused for a moment, smiling so large her eyes squinted almost shut. Her hand reached out blindly for mine, I took it and pressed a chaste kiss to her fingertips. "Wanted to put that to rest before we went searching for the actual answer."

"Well aren't you taking the high road?" She leaned in and kissed me anyway. We'd talked about the necessity of this kiss. Long and sweet and potentially our last. What made me tear up as I pulled back was not the weight of that thought, it wasn't the way Harper was clutching my hand like a lifeline, it was that the kiss was so wonderfully unremarkable. We'd been pouring all our love into our gestures for so many years that there wasn't any feasible way to up the ante anymore.

So we both kissed our long-discussed kiss. Gave ourselves time for a few hundred more kisses before the sun had sunk well below the waves, behind the Earth.

Harper took a slow, deep breath, leaning forward enough to check the small command central we'd built into our ship. Didn't want to have someone stay behind on land in case something went wrong. Didn't want to bring anyone into this that might go running to the proper religious authorities to figure out some kind of lawsuit. So we'd played it risky.

"All right. Let's get this show on the road."

"The high road?"

"Literally, yeah. You ready?"

We'd both hunched towards each other. We were used to checking and rechecking our work. At this point, though, there was nothing more to check. I'd figured I was so familiar with this ship that anything wrong with it was long-past looked over, unfixable now. I'd figured Harper knew her calculations like the backs of my hands.

There was nothing else left to do but fly.

I barely remember liftoff. I figure I got so nervous that I shut my eyes, because all I could remember was squeezing Harper's hand one last time before I had to retreat to my own seat, half a second before the noise crashed down over the two of us. I'd known it was nothing compared to the sound outside—we had the walls of our haphazard ship protecting us from the worst of it—but it was louder in the way wooden rollercoasters are louder. The sensory overload of the shaking plus the roar had made it all seem as if a hundred decibels were added.

By the time I'd opened my eyes, we were well into the sky and Harper was grinning like she'd won the lottery. The sky had gone a dull smog-yellow, lit up from city after city. Looking impenetrable. Even if I knew it wasn't a physical cloud, even if I knew for a fact that we wouldn't be knocked off course from turbulence, my breath had still caught in my throat as I looked up at it through the small rein-forced window we'd built.

It was so much easier to fear death than what came after death, what simultaneously was and was not lying behind the fog of sky.

Our clunker cleared the smog after ten tremulous minutes. Steadied itself to float for the calculated time of one orbit around our washed-out Earth. I'd closed my eyes again, I think, because I didn't look out the window until Harper touched my cheek, light and reverent.

We'd timed it perfectly. Our ascent. The sun behind the earth based on the church buses' travel times. No doubt the light of one angel so close to us would drown out any potential of the rest of them if we weren't careful. We'd been so fucking careful through every detail of this.

I'd reached for her before I looked. And, hand in hand, we saw angels.

I'd been expecting one or two if we were lucky. Spread out among the vacuum, a length of forever between them. I'd expected an af-terlife where I would only see Harper out of my reach once in a blue moon, in a black sky.

The reality is this: there are so many beautiful souls in the world and outside of it. There are angels spread throughout the sky, just out of reach of the ground. Our universe is swirled with light and fire, and all of this was merely what our very human eyes could see.

We had ninety minutes up there. Miraculously, I didn't cry all that much. Laughed and laughed and drowned in joy, yes, but there were very few tears. Harper cried, though. These great, relieved sobs that shook at her shoulders. I don't think I realized until then exactly how much she'd had riding on this one extended moment. Probably was so busy soothing me that she didn't realize it herself, either. We had enough oxygen in the system to sustain all those gasping breaths. It was safe to express.

Our ship came full circle, one complete orbit, and then the thrusters stuttered to life. It was only then that I truly cried, like I'd known I would. Leaving the angels behind was so much harder than seeking them out in the first place. Letting them fade behind the yellow-faded murk of the night was almost physically painful. I don't know quite how long the return to Earth took. I kept my eyes trained on the temp measurements instead of the timer. Had to let go of Harper again. Couldn't speak. The angels had stolen both of our voices away. There was nothing more that could be said anyway.

All that was left was to make sure we didn't burn to death. Or crash, or drown, or any number of things that could kill us if we'd gotten a single measurement or calculation wrong.

But the angels were real. The stars were as real and bright as they were spoken of in prayers, and maybe that was why all I did in those last few seconds before touchdown was close my eyes and whisper up a thanks.

And nothing went wrong. Not dangerously so, at least. I had trouble inflating my life jacket, but our raft sprung to life, and it was sturdy and safe, and the waters were almost monotonous in their predictability. It all felt unreal. I can't describe it well enough, and I'm awful sorry for that. Seeing our life's work sink below the waves, travelling back to shore in the dead of night with nothing but our knowledge and one good life jacket and the hope that no one in the area called the cops on our unregistered ship? It should've been more poignant. All that felt meaningful to me in that moment, though, was that I still had Harper with me. And I would still have her with me when this was all over.

I didn't realize how quiet my mind had become until we reached shore, the hiss of sand slipping over the raft bottom guiding the both of us to step onto land and fetch our computers again and wheel them to the truck on a dolly. And Harper slid her hand around my waist.

"Awful nice night out," she said, still rubbing the saltwater from her face. Tears and ocean water combined. I leaned my head against her shoulder and fished out the plastic-wrapped tissues I'd saved in my pocket. Lavender scented.

"Pretty stars," I agreed. I didn't so much see Harper look to the sky as I felt her shift upwards. Let out a slow, shaking sigh. "They're still out there." I said that quieter, trying to remind myself of it too. "Just because we can't see them doesn't mean they've vanished."

"That cat sure got the short end of the stick."

I laughed again. Told my baby to get in the truck before we spent all night looking up at the sky. Waited to see if any one of our neighbors would report us for some bullshit unregistered spacecraft charge; waited for the statute of limitations to run out.

Well, my friends, it's been quite some time. I figure Harper and I are in the clear enough to post the details of it all. We took a few long-exposure photographs while we were up there. You'll find them attached to this post. The prayer circles are surprisingly accurate, actually. Share the photos with your friends, your lovers, your family, spread them faster than any authority of the church can try to take them down.

Let the world know of the stars.

Maddy Dietz is a high school student who has been telling stories since she learned how to talk. She has lived near major cities her entire life so naturally an anthology raising awareness about light pollution means the world (and the sky) to her. She is an alum of the 2017 and 2018 Alpha Science Fiction, Fantasy, and Horror Workshop for Young Writers and is attending the Juniper Institute for Young Writers in 2019.

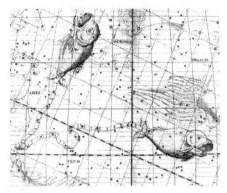

A WEAVE OF EUROPA

MANNY FRISHBERG & EDD VICK

We always thought the gods would be like us, facets of a whole, a living unity. Foolish to imagine so. They exist in the Beyond, outside the hard shell of the universe in which we swim.

We believed that the mothers of our mothers' mothers joined the gods to fly with them in a sea without bound, through endless peaceful tides. We pray that as we prepare for our lifeless bodies to sink to the Deep Below, we may sing the Liberation Song that would buoy us up through the top of the world, adding ourselves to their Weave.

Then they came.

From below, we extended our sail fins to caress the ripples of the gods' modulating emanations, composing our own song in counterpoint. They ignored us. They entered the universe, but without joining it. Their bow wave was a hardness surrounding them like a shell, a duplicate of the universe-shell: a barrier as unyielding as the boundaries of cold solidity enclosing our universe.

We surrounded the gods and sang our joy at their visit, We invited them to join our Weave. Singing to them, we learned their shell was but a thing to contain them, carrying a tiny ocean in which they swam. The gods were incapable of joining the unity of the sea, a tragedy almost too great to contemplate.

At first we supposed this horror had befallen them, that they had been cursed, cast out of Paradise, a shell grown round them to keep them from their Weave. As we would with any who had lost their way, we lamented their fate, sang out and formed knotted loops of sorrow and compassion.

Their song rippled out in all directions with a strange rhythmic beauty. But it had no harmony. It was all power and cadence, harsh waves colliding erratically with no life, no give.

We chanted a new descant to interweave with the gods' dominant beat. The beauty of the new song overlaying alien emanations soothed the Weave, uniting us in rhythmic ripples. Yet the gods were indifferent to our song. We could not say they were refusing the call. We could not say they understood or heard us. Could our song even penetrate their shell?

Still, the gods pulsed. The presence of such a huge discord rippled through the Weave of the universe, shimmering waves distorting the truths we have sung since the Beginning.

Gaps formed which needed dispersing. The feeling spread from a few to the All, waves of confusion swimming against the current, until the decision-wave formed. We must reach out to the Beyond, to learn how to harmonize with the Song of the Gods. Our unity was charged with this mission.

Though we vibrated with a subtle chord of fear, we went.

We followed the gods as they retreated, up and up, until the Shell of the Universe loomed above us. The current tore at us, patently desirous of sending us toward the Beyond. There were gaps, fissures no unity had dared approach before, clefts where the current carried such force as to tear facet from facet. Yet we saw: the gods were not destroyed, so we followed.

The gods continued to rise, but several in our unity were weakened. The cold attacked us, and we felt our insides roiling in the decreased pressure. We had to stop.

We united our song, narrowing it to a single tone to reach the shell itself, to reflect back its form as our bodies reflect one another's. Then we stopped, gave up emitting, and tuned our unity to listening, seeking the harmony of the Outside.

What we found was enormous. In that swirling tug and pull, far stronger than any we had encountered for as long as songs have been sung, our harmonies tore, scattered in the torrent. The gods passed through a rift at the edge of our universe, as did our song. Our broken songs followed the flow of the universe through the fissure.

The ripples of our weave disappeared save one tiny echo from the gods' departing shell; overcome by the emptiness of Beyond. Wave followed wave, rarely building to a unity, and even such unities were soon shredded as they encountered new waves. Though it tore at our understanding, we continued to listen.

One of our unity died, then another. We sang the song of Liberation as their bodies rose in the torrent rather than falling to their rest. We hoped the gods would be gentle with them. Still, we listened.

We sang, a single tone, sustained and focused, until we could feel it stretching to touch a vast Weave. In response, we heard the first song of the new Age, one of an enormous shell some vast distance away, producing pulse after pulse of energy far beyond our imaginations. And, beyond that Beyond, we recognized another and another still, multiplying enormity, emitting ever more powerful waves of energy.

Returning below we sang of waves filling distant oceans far out beyond the shell, of countless shells that floated in even greater oceans, their ripples extending to encounter still greater shells. And the new wave spread throughout our Weave, a song of ripples, radiating outward from the Center of the Universe.

The gods revealed that our universe floats through an even larger ocean, an ocean of oceans. The new universe is an immense Weave of Weaves without end. And beyond, ever vaster oceans, spreading to a far greater Beyond that our songs can never fill.

Edd Vick and Manny Frishberg have written separately for their whole lives and together since 2015. A bookseller and recovering journalist, they have foisted more than six dozen short stories and novellas on an unsuspecting world, alone and together, ranging from hard science fiction to urban fantasies and weird western stories, available wherever fine words are sold (including More Alternative Truths [B Cubed Press] and Analog).

When not editing other people's books, Frishberg is working on his three-book SF/Fantasy mystery series, and Vick is finalizing his first short story collection, Truer Love. Find them at eddvick.com and mannyfrishberg.com.

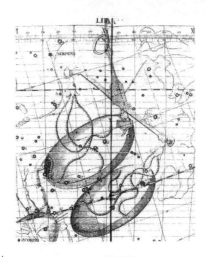

Eleven Tips for Hikers Wishing to Enjoy Moonblossom Trail, Presented by the Antrean Department of Commerce & Tourism

Jamie Lackey

Welcome to Antrea! We're delighted that you've made the trip to our planet. Many of our guests have expressed an interest in hiking our beautiful Moonblossom Trail, so we have prepared this helpful list to ensure that your hike is as enjoyable and as safe as possible.

1. Do not leave the trail.

The trail is blazed with phosphorescent pink paint. Our simple blazing system is explained on signs at the base of the trail. We also offer a trail guide for purchase that includes a helpful map. If you do leave the trail, the Antrean Department of Commerce and Tourism takes no responsibility for the consequences.

2. Photography is strictly prohibited.

Moonblossoms have never been successfully photographed, as their delicate beauty can only be observed with the naked eye. All camera equipment is strictly prohibited on the trail. That does include any personal communication devices that have the ability to take and store photographs. If you'd like a memento of your hike, souvenir art prints and etchings are available throughout Antrea.

3. Wear warm, comfortable clothes.

The best time to see our famous moonblossoms is when all three moons are in the sky. Since the trail is in the southern hemisphere, that means that you'll want to make your trek in the dead of winter. It gets incredibly cold, especially in the high mountain passes, so be sure to wear layers. You can purchase ethically sourced furs and woolen garments from many of our fine shops, so worry not if you aren't able to come prepared—we can help!

4. Make sure to give yourself plenty of time.

The trek up the mountain takes experienced hikers over three hours to accomplish. Novices or those unfamiliar with the climate can easily take nine to twelve hours to make the ascent. You'll want to make sure to set out no later than sunset. Our winter nights are long, but you won't want to rush. There are many beautiful sights to savor! And don't forget to allot time for the hike back! The Antrean Department of Commerce and Tourism takes no responsibility if you are still on the mountain when the sun rises.

5. Be mindful of the weather.

Hiking conditions are posted nightly, but winter storms are often unpredictable. The hike is most beautiful on clear nights, and we recommend that you not venture forth in any sort of inclement weather conditions. The Antrean Department of Commerce and Tourism takes no responsibility for the weather or for issues caused by it.

6. Know your limits.

The Moonblossom Trail is a strenuous hike, and once you begin you will not be able to turn around. Be sure that you are up for the entire trek before you begin. If you are sick or injured or in any way infirm, then you should not hike the Moonblossom Trail. Antrea is full of many other delights that people of all health and fitness levels can enjoy! Health screenings are available, but the Antrean Department of Commerce and Tourism does not guarantee their accuracy.

7. Do not carry food.

While snacks are usually a must on a long hike, they are not recommended for those on the Moonblossom Trail. Our most dangerous predators are diurnal, but you don't want to tempt them with the scent of dried meat or fish or fruit. Be sure to have dinner at one of our many fine restaurants before your hike, and don't forget to carry enough water! The cold air is very dry, and dehydration is no hiker's friend. Branded hydration packs and water bottles are available for purchase from the Antrean Department of Commerce and Tourism.

8. Artificial light sources are prohibited.

Allowing your eyes to adjust is key to enjoying the full splendor of the moonblossoms at the summit. Artificial light is also harmful to much of the flora and fauna that make their homes on our picturesque mountains. Remember, the best time for the hike is when all three moons are in the sky, so there's no lack of natural light! If you're worried about your night vision, you can always hire a guide to help you up the trail. Be sure to select one that is approved by the Antrean Department of Commerce and Tourism.

9. Do not disturb the wildlife.

All good hikers know to leave things as they find them, but that is especially important on the Moonblossom Trail! Contact with the wildlife can lead to unexpected consequences ranging from skin rashes to disembowelment. You can purchase a handy guide that ranks our flora and fauna from most to least dangerous—but even if something isn't dangerous, you should still leave it alone. The Antrean Department of Commerce and Tourism takes no responsibility for injuries or ailments inflicted by local flora or fauna.

10. Do not linger among the glowing mushrooms.

Antrea's glowing mushrooms are as beautiful and celebrated as the moonblossoms themselves. They grow in all seasons, and light the night with the gentle green of their natural phosphorescence. However, their spores can cause drowsiness, so it is recommended that you enjoy their beauty while on the move. Do not give in to the temptation to nap in the snow, no matter how soft and inviting it appears. Filter masks are available for purchase, but the Antrean Department of Commerce and Tourism does not guarantee their efficacy.

11. Do not attempt to interact with the moonblossoms.

You may, of course, look at the moonblossoms. They are what you hiked up the mountain for, after all! However, looking is all that you should do. Do not touch the moonblossoms. Do not smell the moonblossoms. Do not speak to the moonblossoms. Seeing them should be enough for you. Their gentle light is a beauty unlike any other, and the difficulty and danger of the hike means that every hiker fortunate enough to view them becomes part of an elite group. The Antrean Department of Commerce and Tourism takes no responsibility if you do attempt to interact with the moonblossoms.

Eleven Tips for Hikers...

If you follow these 11 simple tips, your hike up Moonblossom Trail is guaranteed* to be both enjoyable and safe. If you'd like more info about the trail, you can check out one of the many books that the Antrean Department of Commerce and Tourism has published on the subject! You can also find more safety tips from pages 512-678 in the mandatory waiver that you signed when you arrived on Antrea.

And remember, there's no shame if you find that you're not capable of hiking the Moonblossom Trail. Antrea offers many other enjoyable activities, and you can always visit the Moonblossom Museum, which is dedicated to artists' depictions of our famous flowers! Thanks again for making the trip to our lovely planet! We hope you enjoy your stay!

* The Antrean Department of Commerce and Tourism guarantees neither your enjoyment nor safety.

Jamie Lackey lives in Pittsburgh with her husband and their cat. She has had over 150 short stories published in places like Beneath Ceaseless Skies, Apex Magazine, and Escape Pod. Her debut novel, Left-Hand Gods, is available from Hadley Rille Books, and she has two short story collections available from Air and Nothingness Press. In addition to writing, she spends her time reading, playing tabletop RPGs, baking, and hiking. You can find her online at www.jamielackey.com.

THE GIRL WHO STOLE THE SUN

J.A. PRENTICE

In a time before the years were numbered, on a moonless night when all the land was an ink-black sea, Leida was born. When she sprung from the womb, so dark and small and silent was she that her mother mistook her for a shadow and left her behind upon the rocks.

Leida grew, yet still was dark and small and silent. Her feet left no marks, even when she walked in mud, and made no sound, even when she walked on gravel. Her clever hands could open any gate and she could make herself seem like anything she wished: young or old, male or female, beautiful or ugly. None knew what form she had been born in, but when she was at ease, she wore the face of a beautiful girl, slightly-built, with dark skin and flowing black hair, so "she" is what they called her.

The people hated her. She was a night-thing, an aberration, a creature not worthy of love. Even her mother had left her alone in the dark, crying out for help that would never come.

So, she became a thief. And because Leida did nothing by halves, she became the greatest thief the world would ever see.

She stole the legs from snakes (for it made her laugh to see them wriggle), the languages of all the beasts of field and sea (the birds she left alone, for she found their language too beautiful, even if no man nor woman could comprehend it), the daytime stars (she missed the morning star, which hid from her behind a low hill), strength from the old (the old had never been kind to her and her heart was bitter against them), and heat from the night (for she loved the cold and the night was her time). These and many other impossible things she did, laughing all the while, wearing her many skins.

But one day, Leida found something she could not simply steal.

There was a woman. Her father was a god of beauty, her mother a great warrior. Her hair was as spun gold, her eyes as diamonds. Her smile was as spring warmth, her laugh was as a campfire on a cold winter's night. All who beheld her loved her.

She was named Glystra for the way she shone.

Glystra was crowned in silver and set upon a high throne. All the peoples of the earth felled forests and uprooted hills to make the walls of her golden hall. A thousand knights pledged themselves her bond-servants, swearing to die for her.

She did not have to fight anyone. What Glystra wanted, Glystra received. All bowed before her, stricken with her beauty.

And Leida was stricken most of all.

She put on her most pleasing form and a raven-feather dress studded with all the stolen day-stars. And in this way, she came to Glystra's hall and bowed low before the lady, most beautiful of all in the land.

There were whispers and murmurings amongst the tables, for all despised Leida, the night-thief, the shape-changer, the trickster.

"Have nothing to do with her," said Glystra's advisor. "She is poison."

Glystra had known nothing of struggle, nothing of darkness, nothing of challenge. Her life was dull as only perfection can be dull, her loves empty as only unearned love can be empty.

Looking up the dark form of Leida, she saw a sort of beauty that was strange to her, sparkling with danger, like the beauty of a well-crafted blade.

If this is poison, she thought, *I would know its taste.*

"Speak," she said. "What is your desire, Leida Night-daughter?"

"You," answered Leida. "Only you, fairest of all the things in the world."

Glystra sighed, for this was of no interest. All creatures adored her.

Even wolves would not touch her, for they were so struck with her beauty they became tame at a look. This Leida, this promise of beautiful darkness, was more of the same.

"I would give you any gift for your hand," Leida said. "I am the greatest thief in all the world. I stole the sound of unwatched trees falling. I stole beauty from the toads. I—"

"The Sun," Glystra said. "Bring me the Sun and I will wed you."

The Hall laughed and Glystra looked at Leida's face, to see what sorrow this challenge had wrought there.

But Leida was smiling.

"Then I will bring you the Sun," she said, and with a last, sweeping bow, she was gone.

Glystra returned to her feasting, but the thief's night-dark face hung still in her mind. In her world of unblemished light, she longed for the beauty of a single shadow.

At every dawn, the Sun came forth from the endless dark beyond the oceans to make war upon the Night. It was a gleaming golden globe drawn by six white-flanked stallions and its light was unbearable. Before it flew a flock of herald birds, bright-feathered, who sang songs of resounding, ear-splitting joy for the coming of day. Heralds and horses alone could journey beyond the oceans at world's end, riding the secret winds.

In the grey time before dawn, Leida sat upon the peak of the highest of the eastern mountains, made herself unseen, and waited for first light. As the herald birds flew overhead, she set her sights upon one red-plumed bird, straggling behind the rest, and saw the glimmer of loneliness in its eye. It alone had no mate to fly with, no nest to return to. It dwelt ever in a bleak, endless twilight from which it could not slip free.

And Leida played three perfect notes upon her flute, the call of a lonely songbird. Seeing no danger, the bird fluttered down and alighted by where she lay, looking for the source of the song.

Leida's quick fingers slipped out, grabbed the bird by the neck and twisted. It lay dead upon the mountainside, its eyes like black glass.

The rest of the flock flew on, on to the west, and the Sun came behind them, accompanied by thundering hooves. They saw neither fallen herald nor thief and spared not a thought for either.

When they had gone by, Leida set about plucking and sewing. Her needle was thin as hope in midwinter and strong as blood-brother's bond. When its work was done, Leida donned her stolen wings and made her shape like a songbird, red-winged and black-beaked. She soared from the mountaintop, carried upon the secret wind, and made her way east across the last sea.

It stretched below her, half-water and half-shadow. In its depths stirred coiling, writhing things—the children of gods, deemed so terrible they had been cast to the edges of the world, where none would see them and none would think of them.

Leida did not look at them as they called to her with wordless voices. Shutting her ears to their lamenting, she flew on.

The waters dwindled until only shadow remained, vast and endless and cold. At its edge rose mountains of silver and gold, from which jutted lighthouses of ancient stone, topped with radiant flames. This was the Harbor of the Sun, where the white horses were stabled and the bright heralds nested.

In a crescent bay rose the Sun's Hall. It was made not of the wood of felled trees, but of living oaks bound together, their twisting roots sinking deep into the earth, their branches entwining in a peaked roof.

Leida flew between two ancient oaks, their bark like scorched rock, and hid amongst the leaves, waiting in the darkness for evening to bring the Sun. There she drifted off to sleep.

In her dreams, she saw her mother, but her back was turned and Leida could not see her face. She ran to her, but the more she ran, the further away her mother was, until a great black sea roiled between them and dread things rose up, terrible and pitiful. They called to her, "Sister!" and hot tears ran down her cheeks.

Song awoke her—the song of the herald flock. Horse hooves pounded against the darkness. The Sun was drawn into the hall—so bright that there were no shadows left, not even amongst the roots of the trees. It was tall as mountains and wide as oceans. Even if Glystra's hall were a hundred times as high, it could not hold it.

This did not trouble Leida, for she knew many spells. In the dark, gods and wizards spoke secrets to the night, believing nobody was listening. But Leida heard every secret whispered in the shadows, every spell, every stolen kiss, every confession, and she forgot none.

The horses shirked their harnesses and rode away, to stables in the mountains where they would find oats and water. The heralds fluttered off into the rafters of the hall, where they nested amongst leaves and branches, their songs dwindling as they fell into sleep.

Only then did Leida creep out from behind her pile of leaves. She tapped thrice upon the Sun and it became small as her hand, though it shone no less brightly. She slid it into her pocket and then flew from the hall, silent as a windless desert.

Laughing, she flew back across the last sea and across the spires of the mountains. Starlight gleamed on her blood-red wings.

When she came to Glystra's hall, it was the dead of night and all was shrouded in shadow and silence. Glystra alone was awake. She stood upon the steps of the hall, looking out into the night and listening to nothing. In the night, there was no cheering, no laughter, no clapping, no confessions of love, and no adoration.

Only in nothingness did she feel anything.

Leida stood in the darkness, watching Glystra. She who had dared to pass beyond the last sea was afraid to take a single step closer.

Glystra turned and saw Leida.

"You're back," she said.

"I am."

"Did you bring me the Sun?"

Leida reached into her pocket and pulled out the golden orb, gleaming bright with inner fire. Glystra's gaze flickered down and she sighed, her breath turning to mist in the chill night air.

"Then I am yours," said Glystra with a bow.

She clapped her hands together and the hall awoke at once, her courtiers and warriors scurrying to her side, begging to know how they might help.

"Set the Sun in a necklace of gold and silver," commanded Glystra. "And make ready the hall. Tonight I will be wed."

There were tears, gnashing teeth, and lamenting. Men and women alike threw Leida glares that could corrode iron. Yet they followed Glystra's commands, for they loved her too much to deny her anything.

Before the whole congregation, Leida and Glystra exchanged vows.

"To ocean's edge, I would follow you," said Glystra.

"In fire, I would join you," said Leida.

"In night, I will lay by you," said Glystra.

"In day, I will stand by you," said Leida.

"In battle, I fight by your side," said Glystra.

"In peace, I honor you," said Leida.

"In all things," finished Glystra, "we are bound, as though by chains of bronze."

"We are bound," whispered Leida.

With a silver-hilted dagger, they cut their palms, tracing red lines across their skin, and let blood mingle with blood. They were one blood, one body, one mind, one soul, for then and forevermore.

Around Glystra's neck, the Sun shone bright, and in the Heavens, there was the rumbling of thunder, though there were no clouds.

Leida led Glystra away into the shadows of the rolling hills. They stood in the long grass, lit by the stars.

"You don't have to," Leida said. "I know you said you would, but—"

Glystra put a hand on her cheek. "But I said. And I want to."

"I can take any form you wish." Leida was a prince, tall and fair. "I can wear any face." She was a hunter, pale and rugged. "Any skin."

"I have seen enough of false, fair things. Wear your own skin."

Glystra pressed her lips against Leida's dark ones and they tumbled back into the long grass.

Every beat of her heart was thunder; every touch of her fingers was lightning; every hot breath against her skin was a hurricane. Together they rode the storm and felt it burning in their veins.

After, they lay in the grass, feeling the blades tickle their sweat-soaked skin.

"When you saw me," said Leida, "you seemed disappointed. I thought..."

"I didn't truly want the Sun," sighed Glystra. "I wished to know what it was to want something I couldn't have."

"I'm sorry."

"When you have everything," Glystra said, "you have nothing. And when you can do anything... you might as well do nothing at all."

Leida was silent for a moment. Then, "Perhaps I could hate you. If that's what you wanted."

"No." Glystra shook her head. "That would be worse. To have hate only because I wanted it. Another wish granted. Another person denying themselves to give me what I desired."

Leida smiled. "I'm glad. I would have found it very difficult."

"If you could give me true hate," Glystra said, her voice soft, "then that would be a gift greater than all the gold in the hills of the earth."

And they lay there together, in the dark of the night.

At last, Glystra said, "This is wrong. Dawn should have come by now."

She was right. It had been hours, and the sky was still black. The stars twinkled out, one by one, till only shadow remained. The Moon was gone and the sky loomed like an endless black maw. All the land was unnaturally still and silent. No animal stirred and the flowers had turned their faces from the sky. A chill wind blew through the trees.

"We need to get back to the hall," Glystra said. She clutched at the burning disc hanging from her neck.

Leida nodded and together they ran across the dark hills towards Glystra's hall, no stars or Moon to light their way, the shrunken Sun pulsing bright on Glystra's chest.

The Hall seemed to be made of shadows. Even the throne, which once had shone with even the slightest kiss of moonlight, was now dim and lightless. All the people cried out, clutching at the hem of Glystra's dress as she passed.

"Doom!" a courtier cried. He pointed a shaking finger at Leida. "Leida Night-daughter, Leida Sun-thief, you have brought doom upon us all!"

"My crops wither," said a farmer. "They grow grey and dry. At the slightest touch, they turn to showers of dust, caught upon the wind and then whisked away."

"Wolves roam free," said a warrior. "They hunt the hills and carry off sheep and babes without the slightest fear. They say the King of Wolves has crawled out of his den, vast and terrible, and he is devouring the forests of the north."

"I cannot work," said a weaver. Her hands were red with needle-marks. "I cannot see the needles. I cannot see the thread. I see only night, endless night, starless night, wherever I look."

Glystra pulled Leida close. "This is not Leida's fault," she said. "She did only as I asked. It was I who asked her to steal the Sun, I who brought this doom upon us."

There was silence, then whispers, then murmuring, then a roar. In the dark, they could not see her beauty, only the shadows she made.

"Glystra has cursed us! Glystra has failed us!"

And the people came at Glystra and Leida in a wave, hands grasping, weapons pointing, but the blaze of the Sun around Glystra's neck was so great that they were blinded. Leida caught Glystra's hand and bore her away, passing like a wind amongst them.

Upon a high hill, they watched as the mob tore down Glystra's hall. Timbers splintered; doors burst; fires blazed. Black ash drifted in a black sky.

Glystra remembered the taste of fine wines that now burnt in their barrels, the scent of roses that now crumbled to ashes, and the warmth of friendly smiles now turned to cold glares. She sank to her knees. Hot tears streaked across her ash-stained cheeks.

"I'm sorry," Leida said.

But Glystra laughed through the tears. "They hate me. You made them hate me."

"You've lost everything."

"No," Glystra replied, her eyes red-rimmed. "I have found Loss."

And Glystra kissed Leida under the shadowed skies, the Sun hot against her chest.

There came a sound like the breaking of mountains and the earth trembled. Glystra clutched at Leida's hand.

Like an eggshell, the sky split. Lights in unnamable colors shone through and strange winds roared across the land.

In cloaks made of storm clouds, riding upon chariots the size of halls, came the gods. They circled round Leida and Glystra and their faces were as fire and sea and jungle and a thousand other wild things. Beneath them, the grass died, the trees blackened, the rivers turned to steam. Glystra fell to the ground, clutching at her burning eyes.

But Leida stood her ground, though her vision swam with scalding tears and black spots.

"Daughter of the Night," said a voice deep as the foundations of the Earth, "you have torn all creation asunder."

"I have done what I have always done," Leida said, "I have gotten what I wanted by stealing, for otherwise I would have nothing."

"The seas thirst for sunlight," said a god made all of ocean waves. Within him swum sea creatures and his brow was capped with a crown of coral.

"I thirsted," replied Leida, "and you never gave me water."

"Children cry out for fear of wolves," said a god made of soft, pink smoke. She smelled of warmth and home and family.

"I cried out," replied Leida. "And you never comforted me."

"Farmers starve," said a god made of tangled branches. Bees buzzed around a wild beard and birds nested on his brow.

"I starved," replied Leida, "until I learnt to steal."

"Enough!" bellowed the first god. "You are a creature of the dark, Leida. We should never have let you torment this world so long."

"I am what you have made me," said Leida. "I have never claimed to be anything else. I have never had a chance to be anything else."

"The Sun shall be restored," the ocean god thundered, and Glystra's necklace tore from her neck and into his hand.

He cast it into the skies and there was a burst of light. Black turned to blue and all the shadows melted away, replaced by brilliant midday. Birds chittered in the trees, joyous to see the Sun again. Flowers turned their petals sunwards, drinking in the light they had been denied.

"Day is once more," said the branched god. "But you will not walk in it, Leida Night-Daughter."

"You shall be cast to the Outside," said the soft god. "Where you will wander the endless dark alone. No more shall you trouble any mortal."

"No." Glystra rose and gazed upon the faces of the gods, though it made tears of blood run down her cheeks. "She shall not go alone."

"Think on this, child," the soft god whispered. "Is she worth enduring the void? Is she worth casting away your life? Your beauty? Here, you are loved by all."

"There," Glystra said, "I shall be loved by her. And her love is of more worth to me than all of creation."

"Then so be it!" cried the first god.

There was a crash of lightning and the sky shimmered. Then a door appeared, a door made of solid night, marbled with ribbons of stars.

"You don't have to do this," Leida whispered.

Glystra took her hand. "I do."

And together, they stepped through the door, out into the boundless void beyond the world. The door shut behind them and was gone. The twittering of sparrows and the babbling of brooks filled the sun-drenched day.

And the world went on, day after day, night after night. Never again was anything seen of Leida or Glystra.

Yet still around fires in the dead of night, people tell the story of the girl who stole the sun. And still, beyond the skies, beyond all the limits of the world, Leida walks with Glystra across the face of the dark.

J.A. Prentice was born in Surrey, but has lived most of his life in America. In 2017, he graduated from San Francisco State University. When he was five, he was attacked by a monkey, which annoyingly proved to be the most interesting thing to ever happen to him.

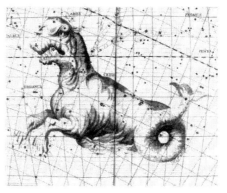

REACHING OUT

ESTELLE RODGERS

I was less surprised when the octopus in tank 19 communicated with me than I would have been if, say, the bivalves had done it. At least in the case of the octopus, the scientific community had pre-existing evidence of incredible intelligence, and many, including myself, suspected personalities in the precocious beasts. So, although I was absolutely astounded by events, it wasn't as if I hadn't secretly considered it a possibility.

Working at a city aquarium is a lot less fun than you think. It's much less high-fiving seals and substantially more cleaning up poop. So much poop. I won't go into excessive detail, but there were just under three-thousand individual residents at my place of employment and they all shit at least once a day. At least. The aquarium tanks were designed to be relatively self-sufficient, allowing for certain natural chemical cycles to occur in restricted confines, but we still needed to change filters and clean the glass regularly. If we didn't intervene, eventually the buggers would clog and cloud the tanks up so badly they'd suffocate in their own waste, and that sort of thing was bad for business.

As a junior hire at the aquarium my first few months of introductory training included, and were almost entirely limited to, "pre-opening beautification." That phrase is corporatese for traversing the staff-only concrete corridors at four in the A.M. five days a week in rubber gloves and waterproof overalls to clean up you-know-what.

At that appalling hour on that particular morning the only other active staff were a security guard and the folks doing the bi-weekly maintenance of the massive central tank, a process that required SCUBA gear. It was disheartening to know that a promotion would mean I only needed more complicated clothing to clean up fish turds. But until I ascended to "more-expensively-dressed janitor," the open petting pools and smaller tanks were my responsibility. So I was very alone in the hallway behind tanks 15 through 20, a place echoing and silent except for the constant gurgling hum of a dozen water pumps, when it all began.

And it began while I was changing the grimiest of four filters in the pump at the rear of tank 19. The creature lurking right beneath me was so adept at camouflage that I didn't even notice it. Suddenly, with a rattling crash, the mesh grate over the tank was knocked askew from within. Crimson and cream suction cup tentacles exploded up from the water and wrapped around my gloved arm. It was like a scene from an H.G. Wells story, sea monster and all, only on a tiny scale.

I didn't react as dramatically as you might expect, if we're being honest. A lot of people are creeped out by critters like an octopus, but I'd held them before and I think they're sort of cute, in a weird, face-only-a-marine-biologist-could-love kind of way. In response to being assailed, I jerked back in surprise and made a small, "euuaah!" sound, but that was about it. It wasn't the first time a sea creature had surprised me, but it was the first time one had leapt out of the water specifically for an embrace.

"Get- what? No! Get off!" I protested, using my free hand to try to gently peel away octopus tentacles. I could feel the suction cups pulling at the fabric of my sleeves and heard faint popping as they disconnected and reconnected with my rubber gloves. The smell of salty water and algae filled my nostrils. "How the shit did you get out?" I exclaimed in a high voice, frustrated that I was having no success detaching the creature from my arm.

Like an alien from a campy silent horror flick, the octopus did to me the exact thing I've always hoped an octopus would never do: it slapped one of its cold, writhing, wet tentacles right on my face.

I let out a distressed moan. My first instinct was to grab the tentacle and rip it away. *It'd grow back, right?* But I resisted, and then had an overwhelming change of heart. With the octopus coiled around my arm, water dripping from my elbow to the floor, and one surprisingly strong tentacle now gripping my forehead, my attention turned to the grate on the lid of the tank. There, I saw the grate had not been broken but rather the bolts securing the metal frame in place had been loosened. Understanding, I turned and looked down at the creature on my arm.

"You *really* want to get out of here," I said.

Somehow I knew that this was exactly correct. This was an escape attempt and a plea for assistance. It must have worked tirelessly to loosen those bolts. I wondered how many times this octopus had tried this maneuver on other early-morning cleaners only to find them less empathetic to the plight of captivity or less acquiescent to face-slaps than I. Then I thought of the vacancy at the aquarium a month back, the one I filled, and I realized this was probably at least the second attempt.

Feeling an incredible pity for the creature, I stepped down from the edge of the tank, bringing the rest of the mollusk out of the water. It was not an exceptionally large or heavy octopus, weighing about five or six pounds and being of the Cyanea variety—that's the kind you sometimes see on nature shows hypnotically changing the color and texture of its skin—and it lost some girth once out of the water. As I stared at it under the dim incandescent lighting in the long, featureless hallway, the suckers of its tentacle still affixed to my forehead in a pathetic plea for mercy, I was overcome by an immense sense of loneliness and homesick.

"You poor thing," I said aloud. When I imagined myself leaving the aquarium with my new friend hidden in a duffle bag, I felt a glimmer of hope. It seemed like a good idea. It seemed like an amazing idea. It was the best, most just idea I'd ever had in my life. I brimmed with philanthropic pride.

Reaching Out

Suddenly my means of employment seemed trivial. My tiny role at this terrestrial prison became disposable, like it was already in the past. I became fixed on a single goal. Determination overtook all my cautions and anxieties, and apparently most of my sense.

"Let's get you home," I said. The octopus stared at me with its glassy orange eyes halved by rectangular pupils and although it did not and could not physically emote, I sensed a heartwarming joy. I knew I was doing the right thing.

Sneaking an octopus out of an aquarium is childishly simple when the octopus is in on it. I pulled a black plastic trash bag from my trolley of supplies, scooped up some water from the tank, and after a moment of exchanging dubious, inter-species glances, the octopus slid in. I tied the bag off with a loose knot and placed it gently in my mop trolley, which I proceeded to then quietly trundle down the hall. I changed out of my coveralls and back into my street clothing, borrowed the rubber gloves, retrieved my jacket from my locker, and transferred the sloshing trash bag from the trolley to my backpack.

Then, still bursting with determined confidence, I left.

The security guard nodded to me on the way out. No one noticed or cared that I was leaving an hour earlier than usual. Maybe they even admired me for it. Or maybe they saw the suction cup imprint on my forehead and figured I had, like my predecessor, had enough for one day.

Outside it was still dark. The sun wouldn't rise for two more hours that time of year. As I crossed the near-empty parking lot I became acutely aware of the bitter cold; my friend in tow was a tropical creature. The confidence that had expedited our escape from the aquarium faltered, and I began to step hurriedly back to my car. I suddenly felt observed, sure that at any moment I'd look over my shoulder to see incensed, SCUBA-clad pursuers waddling after me in high-kicking flippered fury.

I carefully placed my backpack in my passenger seat and ran the seatbelt through the straps. Then I started the engine, switched on the heated seats, and channeled Chewbacca as I did my best to "fly casual" out of the aquarium's desolate lot.

"Okay, little buddy," I said when we were clear of any of my employer's security cameras, as if they could hear me. "I must be out of my mind because I just kidnapped an octopus. Maybe this is what going crazy feels like. And I got some bad news. You are not going to like the water around here. I'll take you to the beach, because maybe you just want to *see* the ocean, like this is some 'dying wish' thing, but this is New England. And I know you don't know what that is, but it sure ain't Hawaii."

To my only marginal surprise, the octopus emerged from my backpack. It had undone the knot in the trash bag and unzipped the backpack from the inside. It oozed gelatinous and amorphous out of the pack, unravelling its tentacles to sit in the passenger seat like a horrifically ugly, but well-behaved, toddler.

"You little creature," I muttered. I turned off the main road and followed a route that would take us to the closest beach. I knew this octopus would die quickly in the local waters, and that I would ultimately probably end up keeping it in my bathtub for a day or two while I figured out a way to transport it to a tropical locale, but, still, I felt compelled towards the beach.

I parked near the locked gates at Ciarniel beach about a mile up the road from the aquarium. When I turned off the engine, three cupped tendrils reached out and wrapped around my right arm. The octopus climbed aboard the me-express once again and rode me out of the car.

Outside the icy wind whipped bitterly off the ocean. I tucked my right arm, octopus and all, behind the shield of my jacket. Animals like that are exponentially more sensitive to temperature change than humans; a few degrees difference can make them sick, even kill them, in hours or minutes.

The same long tendril rose towards my face and again slapped to my forehead.

"You're gonna freeze," I told the creature. As I approached the gate I began to feel less concerned with the cold and much more concerned with the stars. Standing by a black, deserted beach of coarse sand and stone, I tilted my head back and stared up at the inky heavens.

"Hmm," I muttered. "No stars."

I knew, of course, that there would be no stars, even on a very clear night like this one, because we were so close to the city. I could see only the half moon and two or three of the brightest planets.

All at once, a feeling of existential remorse swept through my body in a wave of grief. My heart gave an alarming thump and I was overcome by dismal heartbreak. A sensation of being the victim of an ironic and mercilessly cruel cosmic joke washed through my mind. I wanted to cry. I started to cry. I started to sob. It was so unfair. The stars were gone. I had come so far, gotten so close, but now I was lost and alone. All my efforts came to nothing. I would never get home and I didn't know where I was and I had no one to talk to and no one who understood me and I was cold and hungry and I missed my family. I was going to die here, miserable and frozen and trapped in solitude, unloved and unfulfilled, consumed by loneliness, regret, and longing, and I didn't even know where the hell I was, and before I died I just wanted to see the damn stars.

The shimmering light reflecting on the distant black waves turned to blurred splotches in my vision. The constant thunder of the tide, the smell of salt and frost, the acrid scent of distant car exhaust and oil and tar, my soaked sleeves, the cold suction cups on my forehead; it all gradually returned to me as I forgot the sky.

I looked down at the withering lump clinging to my arm, my eyes wide and blinking away the remains of my tears.

One nearly inaudible 'pop' at a time, the octopus withdrew its tentacle from my head and curled its arm back to its body. I stood in stillness for a few moments, waiting to see what it would do, or what bright ideas would come to me, but there was nothing.

And then, with my human knowledge and human abilities reinstated, my deep melancholy was replaced by a new emotion: outrage. I was furious. This was so stupid; I couldn't let this wonder of nature die so wretchedly. With a determination fueled by the indignation I consider a hallmark of my species, I decided it was time for a road trip.

The engine started and my headlights illuminated the cold dead dunes outside.

"Buckle up, little buddy," I said, letting the octopus melt back onto the backpack. "You wanna see the stars, I'll get you the stars. It's 32 miles to the only beach I know where you can see the sky at night, we've got a hundred and six minutes 'til sunrise, I'm soaking wet, and I am talking to an octopus!"

Unmoved by my comments, the octopus reached out and turned the dial on the car thermostat up as high as it would go. (That *did* surprise me.) Then it wrapped its arms around the passenger side seatbelt and looked at me with an expression as blank and emotionless as ever. In my mind, I imagined it saying, "Hit it."

And I sped the whole way.

We reached the beach in a record 48 minutes. No traffic, no cops, and the emotions of a telepathic cephalopod's existential crisis burned into my psyche made for an expedient journey.

Again I parked near locked gates, this time by the private beach of my hometown. It was the only place I was certain could provide excellent coastal star gazing.

I wrapped the shivering and sickly octopus in my jacket and cradled it in my arms like an infant. I ran from the car, my bare arms exposed to the cold and my head already cocked skyward as I sprinted past the beach gates.

This beach was untainted. It smelled of rich sand, clean ocean salt, and crisp fresh winter air. The world was gray and blue under the half moon. The grass in the dunes shushed and hushed. My footfall on the boardwalk sounded intrusively loud in the serenity of the abandoned place. With each step I sent a resounding wooden echo over the sand below.

When I crested the highpoint of the boardwalk the Atlantic consumed the horizon. It was shimmering onyx and endless, the low and constant rhythm of the crashing waves making the water seem close.

I looked down at the bundle in my arms. It was still and cold. For a moment my heart sunk and I was sure my little friend was departed.

If only, I thought, it could have at least seen the ocean again.

Then, up from the wrap, came a single struggling tentacle. It was gray and silver in the dim light, and it looked shriveled. Filled with infinitely more empathy than disgust I took the slender arm gingerly in my hand and pressed it against my temple.

At once I looked back to the sky.

There was the star-stippled tapestry of my childhood.

We stared for a long time. I kept that weird bundle of adventure close to my heart, holding its tentacle to my head so as not to lose the connection. The nostalgia for home welled in my heart again. I thought I could see the Milky Way in the corner of my eye, but it seemed to disappear whenever I tried to look right at it. What had been a hazy fog near the city was now a brilliant black window to ten thousand ineffably beautiful worlds. I felt like I could look at them forever and never get enough. I wanted to gaze at them, consume them in my eyes and soul eternally. I hoped the sun would never rise and I could stare for all time, never moving and never aging, and even after that I still wouldn't be able to truly know the stars, or keep them.

Certain stars caught my attention for reasons I didn't understand. I matched them against other stars and waited while conclusions too complex to share were drawn in my arms.

Why a beach, I wondered.

Because, I realized, a moment after I thought it, *a coastline is finite and easy to identify. And, no one's usually about this time of the morning, this time of year.*

"You little *creature!*" I said aloud as realization came to me. A laugh escaped my lungs. I had been wondering why this tropical octopus wanted to go to waters as intolerably frigid as the Atlantic. In retrospect the telepathic emoting should have been a big clue.

"I'm here," I said aloud, to my surprise. I think this was my brain's way of processing the nonverbal eruption of emotion emanating from my swaddled bundle.

"I'm here!" I shouted this time of my own volition. I started to laugh, unable to take my eyes off the stars. Tears welled up in my eyes again, but this time they were tears of joy. I was going home, I thought.

Why? I suddenly found myself wondering. *Why leave? Why now?*

At last I was able to take my eyes off the night sky. I looked into my arms but saw only shadows beyond the tentacle bisecting my vision.

A sensation overcame my thoughts then that something was ending. I thought of the turbid sky over the beach by the city, and how the air had smelled of exhaust. A deep sadness filled my mind, fountaining into a feeling that someone I loved was very sick and near death. The morbid resignation, the anger and denial, the profound sense of loss and despondency in the wake of meaningless death; all these emotions played out in my heart.

"Is someone dying?" I asked aloud.

But it was time to go.

If I had been expecting anything, it hadn't been darkness. A blackness had been expanding in the sky overhead, and I hadn't noticed it until it grew so large that it blocked out the moon. Where the beach had previously been a silver woodcut of shimmering water and thread-fine dune grass, it was now a black shadow. I could see far in the distance where the shadow ended and the silver world resumed, but all around me was lost in the pitch.

Then the world turned silent. The steady crush of the surf faded. The rustle of the wind on the sand stopped. The silence reminded me of the way noise-cancelling headphones generate a kind of negative sound. It reminded me of the echoing hum of the water pumps at the aquarium. Then I heard the small "pop, pop" and felt the cold suction cups detach from my head.

"Wait!" I cried. I wasn't ready to say goodbye; I wanted to continue to share this knowledge and wonder that I had only begun to appreciate and understand.

In the blackness something sank down from overhead, something dark, slender, undulating, and visible only by the way it obscured the distant silver light. I imagined a giant cuttlefish mothership come to gather its lonely traveler, but absolutely nothing I could see or hear supported my ridiculous invention. The long shape, invisible in the non-light, prodded at the bundle in my arms.

I couldn't see it, but I could feel and hear it happening. I knew, possibly via some lingering telepathic connection, that my octopus, if it was indeed an octopus, reached out with all eight appendages and took hold of the dark thing the same way it had taken hold of my arm before.

Leaving my jacket slimy and wet, the last of the warmth fading quickly, the octopus disappeared into the darkness. The long shape it clung to pulled up and vanished. The vast, inscrutable shadow above me receded without fanfare or even apparent regard for gravity. As some final farewell gift, I was given a thought about the light spectrum and all the colors of the universe I could not see with my human eyes.

Then I was alone. Standing on the boardwalk of a frigid New England beach, jacket hanging from my hand, head craned back to gawk uncomprehendingly at the stars. Soon the sun would creep up before me and I would have to return to my car, the city, my life.

I imagined myself as a creature in a giant, spherical aquarium. I pictured all the little humans moving around in their habitats, eating, mating, pooping. I pictured myself, as I was, staring at the stars, unable to remove the grate over my head. I was left there while the filters clogged, the air turned murky, and there was no one I could hail to come lift me up from my filthy, dying world.

Estelle has a great many hobbies, one of which is obviously writing. An abbreviated account of her other pastimes includes: painting, sewing, crafting, photography, cosplay, reading, rescuing turtles, fact-checking, thinking about fish, and looking at the night sky in different countries to see if it feels any different. Those last two are very relevant to her story in this anthology, which, if you've read, means you'll also be unsurprised to learn she grew up in an old Massachusetts town with a nice beach. She's published three short stories and you can find her on Instagram as @estellerodgers and on twitter as @estellewrites.

MAGGIE MATRIX &
THE LONELY MOUNTAIN BAND

JAMES EDWARD O'BRIEN

It had always been Mars in the schlocky old yarns: *Mars* needing women, *Mars* mounting its grand Earth invasion, *Mars*—where humans might have one day dwelt under fishbowl domes in urethane-coated nylon pajamas.

But it turned out to be Ceres, the runt between Mars and Jupiter, that humanity set its thirsty eyes upon. Ceres and its water.

I stared out the freighter's bay window, past the unfinished empty of space. I'd never felt sympathy for goldfish who leapt from the safety of their tanks only to splat against a cold, uncaring floor until I embarked on this six-month journey toward Ceres.

"How you holding up, Maggie?" asked Meyer.

"Holding up," I replied.

After Earth's Potable Water Incursion, what remained was so poorly rationed that it made anything beyond surviving day-to-day far too big a luxury for your average Joe or Josephine. The land of plenty became the land of just enough—scarce demand for harp players among a population preoccupied with staving off the perpetual dry mouth, dizziness, and headaches brought on by dehydration.

The Ceres gig was Meyer's bright idea. He was by no means the best manager, but I was by no means the best player. I just carried the lowest asking price. Persistence spoke volumes.

Meyer chomped on an icicle. The sound of it gave me the heebie-jeebies. "Can I getcha one? I gotta keep my star hydrated. The recycled air in this tin can's murder. My skin's peeling like a cheap paint job." He slurped. "Gotta tell ya, the matcha ones aren't half bad."

"Doesn't it freak you out Meyer, the way it feels like nobody's running this ship?"

"For cryin' out loud, Maggie, you're a bright girl—you'd think you'd be used to it by now. Tell ya what. I feel safer in the hands of an autopilot than I do with the water barons back home. You're just stir-crazy. It *has* been six months, after all."

"So nobody's running the ship *anywhere* when it comes down to it, is what you're saying… and that's supposed to make me feel better?"

"The worst is over. You've just gotta fight through one last day before we hit Ceres."

He meant well, I guess, but I was sick of icicles. I was tired of space. Perpetual darkness pinpricked by the ghost light of dead stars. Fed up with the "luxury suite" bequeathed us by the Intergalactic Endowment for Music Appreciation, a climate-controlled shipping container surrounded by a shantytown of supply crates in the bowels of the freighter.

Ceres Cardinal sat atop Ceres' only mountain. One might think its architects would have made the walls of the atmospheric dome transparent to afford its residents a primo view of the landscape, but the entire complex, with the exception of the glass-roofed odeum housed at its top, was opaque. Onyx. They'd supplanted the blinking, black maw of space with a prefab sky all their own. There wasn't so much as a porthole around the entire perimeter to remind inhabitants of the inhospitable world outside, as if space itself had become a cruel reminder of their defeat—their need to leave home, to abandon their stately mansions and financial advisors and Atlantean snowbird retreats.

Shipping water back to Earth was far too costly, far too inefficient, so those with the means went straight to the source. Having to abandon their earthly comforts was a sore spot for these expats, a reminder that we were all beggars, all refugees in one way or another, and that their material wealth could only shield them from so much.

Water harvesters spread from the base of the mountain as far as the eye could see: machine-pyramids capping the vapor-spewing geysers that pocked grassless tundra. The underside of Ceres Cardinal's dome, however, was lit up in a perpetual state of Diwali. Ceres taught me humans are as much creatures of color, defined by its presence and absence, as we are beasts of insatiable thirst. Vibrant mustards and burnt umbers danced across the vaulted ceilings in defiance of the hollow grays and blank, black sky that dwelt on the other side of the buttressed walls.

By the time the freighter moored and Meyer and I cleared the reclamation chute, a legion of socialites swarmed the arrival gate— mostly trophy spouses of water barony operatives. The show's promoter, Wauneta Nguyen, was waiting for us too. Wauneta's avatar, a she-Martian in a hoopskirt projected in mold-green light just above her head, held a virtual welcome sign with my name on it. Wauneta elbowed her way through the pack of culture-starved *Haus-Ehemänner* and waved me through.

"Ms. Matrix, a pleasure." She extended her hand limply. Her eyes drifted toward my mousy brown hair, her own a bold shock of stop-sign red wound up in a beehive. She scrunched her nose, a meager attempt to hide her disapproval. I noticed.

"Wauneta," crooned Meyer, "even more stunning in real-time than the TV Eye makes you out to be." He leaned in to kiss her. She deflected him with a cheek.

All the hangers-on dyed their hair bold colors too: kelly greens, Mardis Gras purples, electric blues, dandelion yellows—even the bald and balding joined in with what wispy, thinning strands they had left—anything to set themselves apart from the breathless, anemic tundra on the other side of the dome.

"Did you have a good flight?" Wauneta asked.

The carbon fiber casks housing Jerri and Thom-Thom slalomed from the chute behind us, clamoring to the ground like two disarmed torpedoes.

"Easy with the talent, for crying out loud," Meyer warned the stevedore.

If looks could kill, the glare Wauneta gave that stevedore might have dropped him then and there. "Don't worry," she assured us, "I'll have *my* people deliver them straight to the venue."

I felt as if the weight of the world was pressing down on me. I leaned hard into the soundboard of my harp just to stay upright.

Wauneta waved me off. "It's natural. We'll get you to the lodge and get you suited up. You'll feel right as rain."

"Suited up?" asked Meyer.

"It's the city's gravitational modulators. There's a learning curve. We'll size you for exoskeletons—to prevent undue strain on your joints and bones, and compensate for any muscle loss during the trip here. Until you acclimate." Wauneta winked. "I know what you're thinking, Ms. Matrix, and *don't*. Exoskeletons shave a solid decade off your figure. They're *all* the rage up here."

Wauneta had a pair of bruisers in tow. Twins. Clones maybe, I didn't ask. The two women, all corded muscle, Kevlar zip-ups, and neon cornrows, cleared a path through the posse crowding the gate. They ushered Meyer and me from the arrival gate through a series of labyrinthine tunnels until we arrived at the lodge: a gargantuan, metallic hornet's nest of a thing built into Ceres Cardinal's southernmost wall.

Far as I could tell, we were the only guests. They gave Meyer and me adjoining suites. I collapsed on the queen-sized bed and set the room's skin to *20,000 Leagues Under the Sea*. Walls and ceiling erupted in effervescent aquatic blue. Tropical fish navigated the bubbles, ricocheting off one another. I barely had time to kick off my moccasins before Wauneta's tailor sashayed through the door unannounced, two transparent fitting stools in tow.

"Quaint," he snarled, barely masking an eye-roll at my room skin selection. He slapped up the stools in the dead center of the bedroom. "If you please, Ms. Matrix." He gestured toward the seat.

Standing made me weak-kneed. Stars erupted in my peripheries. *Learning curve,* Wauneta Nguyen had said.

The tailor grabbed me by the scruff of my ruff and coaxed me onto the stool. "Is your... uh... *cohort* on premises?" he asked.

"Meyer!" I yelled to the next room.

Meyer waddled in. He planted himself beside me. A fitting-bot ferried in two dressmaker's dummies: adaptive plastic torsos equipped with 3D printing tendrils.

"My bot will let itself out," said the tailor. He curtsied, and was gone.

The fitting-bot's snout emitted a soft, pink beam that scanned me, then Meyer, head-to-toe, calculating our dimensions. Every imperfection.

The 3D printing tendrils whirred as the dummies' adaptive frames morphed into approximations of Meyer's and my own physiques. Tendrils spat, weaved, and clipped the articulated webbing that would constitute our adaptive exoskeletons.

"Did you see the way they look at me?" I hissed to Meyer. "Nguyen and her tailor both—like they're doing *me* a favor. Like *I'm* the apple knocker from the Styx!"

"You got raw talent, Maggie. What do they got? A half-dead planet full of underground icebergs that keep them sticking around for their next fix. You're a musician, Maggie. Music's freedom. These are businesspeople, constantly looking at what they *don't* got instead of what they *have.* Jettisoned up here by their fear of dying of thirst. Art and commerce, kid," Meyer chuckled. "There's always gonna be that push-and-pull, even 400 million kilometers from home."

Meyer cued his avatar. A cartoon terrier in a derby hat materialized above his head.

"Maybe this'll ease your bruised ego. Their second deposit cleared."

8-bit gold coins spiraled above the terrier. They popped like soap-suds as the virtual pup ran circles around Meyer's shiny pate yapping.

"It's just one gig. Once that final deposit clears, you'll be able to swing so much H2O back home that you'll need to graft gills to your cheeks. You'll be back on terra firma by summer solstice."

"I guess thirst *is* the great equalizer," I sighed.

Once the tendrils quit their spinning, the dressmaker's dummies wriggled free of our freshly minted, fully articulated exoskeletons.

"Stand please," requested the fitting-bot—quite sultrily I must admit, for a bucket of bolts. We complied. The tendrils then stripped us and fitted the exoskeletons over our skivvies, before dressing us again.

I felt like a million bucks. Like I could climb the walls or run a marathon. It was getting late, though, so sound check had to do.

The odeum's transparent roof threw me right back into the dull nightmare of the last six months: blank space and stars winking blankly.

I activated the chamber's skin, setting it to Bornean forest, pre-extinction: the patter of raindrops against waxy leaves. Clouded leopards and orangutans regarded me through cautious, ancient eyes.

I rolled the kick drum onto the riser. The drum sprouted toms, snares, high-hat, and a stool. Its drumhead whinnied open. Thom-Thom spilled out of the amniotic goop within: legless torso of a body, handsome face, broad chest, and four muscular arms, each fist clenching a drumstick the way a baby might latch onto its mama's fingers.

"Doing alright, Thom?"

Thom-Thom hacked up a gob of amniotic fluid and pivoted straight onto the drum stool. Poor Thom was a lab-grown, lizard-brained humanoid designed for one purpose only: the beat. The beat. The beat. The beat provided his sustenance: *audiosynthesis* they called it—not far from the way photosynthesis works in plants, minus the need for nutrients, CO2, and all the other bells and whistles.

Why not drum machines, you ask? Machines, as of yet, lacked heart.

I slunk toward the upright bass. I turned the nutrient lamp affixed to its stand up to eleven. Jerri's E-A-D-G strings hummed, ever so gently, down Jerri's fret board, through Jerri's hollow, hourglass body.

Jerri's creator was a tree-hugging plant geneticist who cultivated a sentient strain of wood figuring it'd serve as the spokesmodel for the Earth's disappearing forests. But the agribusiness conglomerates were deaf to all things but the almighty dollar. Jerri ended up a showpiece 'til me and Meyer came along.

"You dig the curtains in this joint?" I asked Jerri, indicating the Bornean forest I'd thrown up to keep the outside out.

Jerri slapped out an "affirmative" in Morse down the G string. Sunlight and rain, forests and freeform jazz—that was Jerri's jam. This rock 'n' roll game was just a way to pay the bills. The way I saw it, rock 'n' roll survived the eons because it's an eternally unfulfilled promise, a sugarcoated impossibility. Youth caught in the eye of time like a gnat in amber.

It took a few flubs before I adjusted to playing suited up in the exoskeleton. I steadied my harp between my legs. I wiggled my fingers, coaxing out the phantasmal strings of silky, concentrated light that concretized from neck to pedestal.

"It'll be a full house tonight," I reminded Jerri and Thom-Thom, as if a hurricane has a care for who's huddled in the barn.

The house lights went up. The crowd went wild. I opened with a Carolan reel. It garnered polite applause. Cretins.

The rhythm section kicked in on the second number. Jerri and Thom-Thom played with the urgency you'd expect from entities whose very life's blood was rhythm, hell-bent on shaking out six months of dormancy. I could barely keep up.

The crowd spilled across the dance floor like a broken bag of rainbow-colored candies. Jupiter edged into view above our heads—a giant, phosphorescent marble pushing the big, dumb, starry void out of the picture.

I sang myself hoarse. We tore through every gin-joint standard, every barn-stomper, every three-chord number in our repertoire. The hall got muggy fast—stifling, in fact—from the heat of bodies in motion.

The harp's glassy reverb shook droplets of condensation from the sky-lit dome until it felt as if all of space and time were raining down upon us, as if Jerri and Thom-Thom's locomotive rhythm and the plucky melody of the harp strings riding its crest were the very forces urging Jupiter across the firmament, the music so infectious it moved planets, too.

Of course I knew all this to be untrue, but, for a split second, amidst this sterile world of geometric calculations, recycled air, water harvesters, and gravitational regulators—*ta-da!*—for one imagined moment, there was magic among us, alive as anything could ever be.

The crowd ate it up. They wanted more. They wanted *transcendence* when all I had left was a voice that sounded as if it had been run through a belt of used ashtrays. My callused fingertips beat like ten tiny hearts.

I cued my avatar. It fizzled to life above my head: a honey-gold harp with a picture-perfect effigy of myself carved right out of the pillar. From my unkempt bob to my winkle picker boots, all golden, a totem shimmering and hollow-eyed.

The crowd watched in awe as the lips of my golden self parted, siren's vibrato accompanying my hurriedly plucked strings. It was all canned, intuitive software, but the crowd did not seem to care; they wanted a smoke-and-mirrors show. Whether anyone sweat or bled for it was inconsequential; the magic had come and gone at its own discretion, and these luddites couldn't tell the difference either way.

Those still seated sprung from their chairs as the final note from Jerri's warped frame resounded in everyone's chests, deep and crippling as a sledgehammer blow. I turned toward the rhythm section and gave them a nod.

The crowd went nuts. Off stage right, Meyer was all smiles, avatar terrier running circles around his shiny pate with dollar signs in its eyes. Beside him, Wauneta Nguyen golf-clapped as she scrolled through the feed on her steno.

There would be after parties. Meet-and-greets. Press junkets for the fans back home, followed by the six-month return through soundless, inhospitable space––too silent a sabbatical, if you ask me.

That's when I envied Jerri and Thom-Thom most. They were spared all that in-between time squirreled away in their carbon-fiber casks, hibernating. But at this very moment, it was as if all three of us had weathered some magnificent storm. As if we'd *been* the storm.

And maybe we *had* turned a couple worlds upside down. But Jupiter still passed unabated and the unwashed masses still pushed toward the exits as if we'd gone invisible. Thom-Thom curled back up in the womb of his kick drum. Jerri's strings fell silent.

Inside Ceres Cardinal the whole wide world wore blinders. But beyond its walls, I reminded myself, there was tundra sprawled out as far as the eye could see, whether anyone wanted to see it or not, quiet and lonely as the odeum past curtain call. And above it, a stormy sea of sky: dark, wild, *magnificent.* Deaf to our song.

James Edward O'Brien grew up in northern New Jersey where he graduated from Dungeons & Dragons to punk rock to Samuel Beckett, all three of which continue to inform his work today. His short fiction and poetry have appeared in InterGalactic Medicine Show, Eye to the Telescope, and on the Tales to Terrify podcast. He lives in Far Rockaway, NY with his wife and three rescue dogs. Follow Jim on Twitter: @UnagiYojimbo.

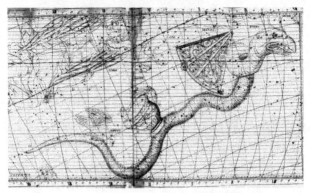

RATTLESNAKE SONG

JOSH ROUNTREE

The Last Picture Show came to the movie house on the square in the fall of 1971. We snuck in with warm cans of Pearl and sat in the back row so we could take quick hits off our cigarettes and snub them out before anyone noticed the smoke. I fell in love with Cybil Sheppard and figured she could wind me up just like she did all the guys in Anarene. I recognized that small town that had been something once upon a time but was now engaged in a battle with time. Every sandstorm, every gust of West Texas wind stripped away another layer of paint and vitality. That dying town was our inheritance.

When the movie ended we spilled out onto Front Street with our half-full beer cans stashed in our jackets. Dean Champion's dad had been a big hat over at the refinery in Big Spring before he hung himself, so Dean had sprung for the beer. We piled into his Chevelle and I made sure I was in the back seat, squashed tight against Stacy Bell's thigh. Once upon a time that prospect would have excited me, but that time had passed.

Dean hollered, "Pass it!" Jason or Holly or Gilbert had produced a pencil thin joint and when it made the rounds to Stacy and she held it out to me, straining to keep the smoke in her lungs a few seconds longer, I waved her off. Things were strange enough without it. The Chevelle's tires squealed, caught the road, and we fled that nothing of a town square.

The night opened up and let us in. Half drunk, I pressed one cheek against the cold window and saw the stars collapsing down from the heavens. They looked streaky and smeared, like someone had gone at them with a washrag. I closed my eyes, felt the hum of the road, the jerk as the car found high gear. A mile or so on, Dean braked and cornered us onto a caliche road. Rocks rattled off the undercarriage. My brain latched on to the possibility of skidding off the road at this speed and flipping over into the empty cotton fields, then the rough scales on Stacy's fingers brushed mine and I found I really didn't care.

"Everyone out!" Dean again.

I hadn't realized the Chevelle had stopped moving.

The car ticked to a stop, and we piled out. If there was a moon, it was afraid to shine in that place. Our feet sank into the soil as we trudged into the fields. Nothing remained of the harvest but dead, crunchy plant husks. Rattlesnakes prowled the rows. It was far too cold for snakes, but that sort of thing hardly mattered anymore.

Dean found a likely spot, dropped to his knees and the others joined him, their hands already digging into the soil, turning it over like they were searching for arrowheads. Connecting with the blood of the place, I guess. Their forked tongues tasted the night. Hands in my jeans pockets, I stood apart, unsteady and unsure why the rattle-snake song affected everyone else, gave them a purpose.

I stared up into the boiling sky. All around us snakes coiled and hissed and rattled and my friends swayed in the blackness, doing their best to join the song. The wind tugged at my farm coat, iced the back of my neck. The desperate scent of Stacy's Woolworth perfume joined the smell of stale beer. I imagined, too, that I could smell the snakes, musty and corrupt, and the whole cocktail brought vomit to the back of my throat.

Dean grinned like a fanatic. His brother had grinned that way once, and now he was in the state hospital. His father too, and they'd found his body swinging from a beam in the garage. Some things were too hard to wrap your mind around.

I couldn't understand the attraction of staring into that terrifying sky, pondering the swirling stars and the coiling strands of colored light, not reds and greens but impossible, unimaginable colors. No human way to describe them without seeing them. But for those who could interpret the rattlesnake song it was a kind of worship. I tensed up when snakes slipped in and out of the circle, even though I knew they wouldn't hurt us. They weren't reptiles anymore; they were heralds of the gods.

After a time, Gilbert and Holly stood in unison, glassy-eyed and still swaying. Dean fished in the pockets of his letter jacket for his keys and Stacey grinned at me before jumping up and heading to the car. They called back half-hearted goodbyes as they got into the Chevelle, leaving me to trudge across the cotton field to my house.

I snuck through the front door, keeping quiet so I didn't wake my parents. Force of habit from the days when they used to care whether or not I was coming in past curfew. On the way to my room, I opened their bedroom door a crack. They were still alive. I could tell by the hissing and heaving of their snores.

We'd made it through another day without the world coming to an end.

A week later I went to see the movie again. I figured I might not have too many more chances to watch movies so I'd better take advantage. The town was closing itself up.

The old men who liked to gather out front of the drug store with their dominoes and long-winded memories had retreated to their houses. Old women abandoned church socials, clotheslines, and ironing boards to embrace the winding down of their lives. The new reality was harder on the older people. They'd had a good long time to dig in their heels on the whole God is Good thing, only to be shown that the universe was terrible and unknowable.

Oh well.

The Dickensons who owned the theater had left the building unlocked and I knew how to run the projector from the summer I'd spent selling tickets and serving popcorn. As the film flickered to life on the screen, I dug my fingers into a bag of M&Ms and wondered if the Dickensons were still alive.

Duane was up on screen hitting Sonny in the head with a bottle when Stacey sat down beside me. "I was looking for you."

"Here I am," I said.

"How many times have you seen this movie now?"

"A few."

"Lot of people having sex in this movie. Do you think everybody in this town is having that much fun?"

I was pretty sure nobody was having fun anymore.

"The movie's not really about sex," I said. "It's about wanting to be somewhere else than where you are and being stuck. They're all just having sex because they don't have anything better to do. They're bored."

"Doesn't sound like the worst reason why anyone ever had sex," she said.

"Why were you looking for me?" I asked.

"Wanted to see if you'd drive out to the fields with us again. It's almost dark. You want to come look at the stars? Maybe you'll hear the song?"

The last thing I wanted was another reminder of the new world order and how poorly I fit in. Stacy cupped the side of my face, gently pulled my gaze from the screen and positioned it on her. I managed not to flinch. Her scaled palm was scratchy and cool against my skin, and the change from who she'd been to whatever she was becoming had picked up speed.

"It's okay you haven't heard it yet," she said. "Don't worry, it'll happen."

I wanted to scream out how I hoped to Hell it never did happen, and how I thought maybe I'd rather die than become like Stacy and the rest of them. How I'd have preferred even to join the adults in their slow insanity and rot. But she held me in place with those blue eyes that I had daydreamed about since middle school. Her stare was heavy and uncomfortable, like she was trying to fanaticize me by force of will. I realized I was afraid of how she might react if she knew how badly I wanted to look away.

"You go ahead," I said. "Tell everybody I'll catch up with 'em later. I want to finish the movie. See if it ends the same way this time."

Stacy gave me a cold kiss on the forehead. "We'll say a prayer for you."

"Appreciate it."

I stared at the screen for another hour, but I wasn't really watching the movie anymore.

That evening, I put my ear against my parents' bedroom door. The house was quiet as a church. I remembered the tears streaking down their faces on that night when the stars changed, the way Mom had fallen to her knees like a load of laundry spilling out of the hamper, and the way the light had passed from Dad's eyes like our new gods had puckered up and blown it out. Maybe the adults were luckier than the rest of us. I thought about opening the door to make sure there was nothing I could do. Instead I loaded up everything I cared to take into the bed of Dad's pickup truck, and moved myself into the lobby of the movie theater.

Within a month the rest of the adults in town were either dead or wandering the roads like children lost in a foreign country. A few of them might have left town, but I didn't know for sure. I hadn't seen anyone who wasn't local in a long time, and I'd decided that the outside world knew instinctively to avoid us. The flip side of that coin was that I didn't think anyone of us was supposed to leave. I'd lived my whole life desperate to be anywhere else, but now I was stuck.

The second story of the movie house overlooked the town square: the turn-of-the-century jailhouse that had been built to hold cattle thieves and rogue Indians, the dusty stretch of stores that hadn't been very lively even before their owners had abandoned them, and the art deco drugstore building that had developed a slight eastward lean over the years, as if it had grown tired of the constant wind and was preparing to give itself up to the world's fury. The town's lone stoplight blinked on and off forever at one corner, and the handful of old pecan trees had shed their leaves and become skeletal hands, fingers spread wide in an effort to hold up the falling sky.

A bonfire burned in the middle of Front Street, one of the only pieces of earth not swarming with rattlesnakes. My classmates strode across this sea of reptiles like Jesus on the water, assured in their new faith. The snakes themselves didn't seem to care. Dean kept gunning his Chevelle up the street and back again, 8-track blasting Black Sabbath, a couple of other kids laughing and whooping in the backseat, and the snakes would part to let him pass every time. Someone had discovered a stale keg of beer in a stalled out delivery truck and the worshipers of our new gods had proceeded to get sloppy drunk. Gilbert and Holly both pounded on the movie theater doors and then called up to the window to invite me down, but I waved them off.

Jason and Stacy were coiled together in a kiss at the edge of the bonfire, and I felt a hot stab of jealousy in spite of myself. That could have been me for sure. But the sensation faded fast, driven off by the clamor of ten thousand rattlesnakes, rising up from the blacktop like the sound of bacon frying in a skillet. That couldn't have been me. Not really. Would I have wanted it to be?

They hovered together in the crosshairs of my Dad's old .208 rifle. I was pretty sure I didn't intend to shoot anyone, but having it there reminded me that the universe hadn't stolen all of my options.

Shooting them all before the world ended might be a mercy. Problem was, I wasn't sure if they were the ones needing mercy, or if it was me.

I got in the habit of slinging that rifle over my shoulder whenever I left the theater. I had it with me one morning in the early hours, when all of my old friends had slunk back to their holes and the snakes had settled into an eerie silence. I picked out a snake that was coiled up on the step of the jailhouse and shot it in the head. The sound of the rifle rattled around the square for several seconds, but none of the snakes stirred.

The morning sun was still an hour away, and the colors in the sky still held sway. They were smeared from horizon to horizon like a kid's crayon drawing, and they felt so much closer than they'd been. Staring at those colors long enough, you could make out patterns. You could begin to see things that you didn't want to see. And yet, once you stared long enough, it became hard to look away, like if you didn't keep an eye on the stars they would crash down and suffocate you.

I might have stared for two minutes or twenty, but I finally shook myself loose, lowered my head and saw every rattlesnake in the square with its head up, staring right at me.

That was enough to put me in motion.

By the time the sun was up, I had Dad's truck loaded with my piss-poor collection of clothes and keepsakes, all the boxes of candy left in the theater, and a few dozen bottles of Dr. Pepper. The morning was cold but the heater cranked right up when I started the truck. The rumble of the engine and the way the seat rattled beneath me reminded me of riding with Dad out to the feed store on the interstate when I was a kid. Country music on the tinny speaker. Dad smelling like sweat and soil. On Sundays I'd squash myself between my parents in the cab on our way to church, Mom with some sort of casserole dish in her lap and Dad with the window cracked to let out the cigarette smoke. Dad only ever went to church to make Mom happy, and I'd quit going with them a few years ago because basically I was an asshole and was only just figuring that out. I closed my eyes and tried to smell that casserole and the fresh, flowery scent of Mom's face powder.

Someone knocked on the truck window, and I nearly pissed my pants.

I was pretty sure it was Dean. He wore his letter jacket, and a few patches of his blond hair remained. He used to wear it a little past his collar just to rile up his coaches, but now what remained of it clung in grass-like chunks to his scaled skull. The rest of him…well, I couldn't have told him from any of the others. When he spoke, it was still his voice. Mostly.

"Where you going, man?"

I rolled down the window and the morning cold chased away my fortress of warm memories. Dean's tongue licked the air, but I'm pretty sure he was smiling. I resisted the urge to gun the gas pedal.

"I think I have to leave town," I said.

"Oh man, don't do that," he said.

"Dean, you know I don't belong here anymore."

"I wish you wouldn't leave." Something in his expression changed and best as I could tell, he looked genuinely sad. "I know you can't understand what the snakes are saying but it don't matter. This is your place, man. Where else would you go?"

I had no idea, but I knew I couldn't stay there any longer. It might have been my place once, but those days were long gone.

"How long before they get here?" I asked. "The new gods."

"Won't be long," he said. "Hard to say for sure but I figure a week or two. We can't change that, you know. Don't matter if you're here or out to California, they're still coming. Better you stay here and we can vouch for you. You're one of us. They'll understand that."

"I don't think they will," I said.

Dean hissed. "We been friends since we were kids. Played Pony League together, you at second and me at shortstop. We worked our tails off last summer stringing that barbwire around old Jameson's cattle acreage. I vouched for you for your parents that night you got drunk at Holly's party and passed out in her backyard. Ain't we friends anymore?"

"Yes, we're friends," I said. "But I still got to go."

All that was kind and soulful suddenly leaked away from Dean's lidless eyes and I thought for a second he was going to yank open the truck door and stop me from leaving. He could have done it. He had my by at least twenty pounds. But instead he backed up and threw his hands up in mock surrender.

"Go then if you got to," he said. "But you got plenty of friends who at least deserve a goodbye."

Might be he was right. But I dreaded the prospect of reliving this same conversation with the others, and I was dead certain that Stacy would convince me to stay. I put the stuttering old truck into gear, steered it past the flower shop, and made the left turn onto the farm road that would eventually take me to the main highway.

My tires rumbled along the caliche road as I accelerated, and for the first time I gave some thought to where I was going. I'd strained against the boundaries of my hometown ever since I'd been old enough to walk. There were a whole lot of interesting places on television and in the movies, and almost all of them looked better than where I was from. But my parents weren't really vacation people. We rarely travelled farther than the next town over, and that was just because their grocery store served better cuts of meat than ours did. I'd only left Texas once. We'd driven out to the mountains in New Mexico when I was ten and I still held the cool pine-scented memories of that place with me through every miserable Texas summer. I still had a pinecone stashed somewhere at my parent's house. If our world had two weeks, give or take, before the new gods arrived, I could think of worse places to spend them than those mountains. Or maybe I could head to the border. Drink some beers on a Mexican beach or check out some of those jungle ruins I read about in one of Dad's adventure novels. It didn't really matter. The prospect of being somewhere other than the handful of dusty streets I'd walked my whole life was right there in front of me, and there was no longer any reason to stay.

When the pain came, it was sudden and bright, like getting stabbed with an icepick. My body recoiled, and my knees caught the steering wheel, yanking it to the right. Before I could correct, the truck barreled off the road and into the bar ditch. One wheel caught a fence post and my head slammed against the roof of the cab as the truck rolled over twice and came to rest on its side, wedged in a nest of angry mesquite trees. Blood colored my vision and my shoulder screamed like it had gone out of joint. The rattlesnake was still latched on to my ankle, letting every drop of venom seep in. I made a halfhearted attempt to shake it loose, but I was caught tight. Frigid wind blasted in through the broken windshield and I could taste the soil in my teeth. My red vision faded to black, and I could hear Dean's reptilian voice taunting me like a ghost.

This is your place, man.

Where else would you go?

I woke in an aluminum cattle trough in the middle of my parents' abandoned cotton field. The trough's brackish water had been emptied and replaced to the rim with rattlesnakes. The winter wind rushed freely across the plain, chewing away the last of the afternoon sun with icicle teeth, but I soaked in that cold reptile flesh like it was warm bathwater. The snakes kept completely still, even as I grasped the side of the trough and pushed up into a standing position. My left arm hung limp and a painful lump had settled over my ear, but I was alive.

My friends circled the trough, watching in silence with their unblinking eyes. That morning I would have screamed to wake up with them staring at me like that, but a surreal calm had taken hold and I realized what had changed. The rattlesnakes were singing, and I could hear their song.

Dean, Stacy, and the others swayed to the writhing, clattery rhythm and when I stepped out of the trough and trudged away through the soil, one ankle swollen twice its normal size, they made no move to stop me. A couple of them started to follow but I waved them off.

"Where are you going?" asked Stacy.

"Don't worry. I'm not leaving. This is my place."

Back in my movie theater perch, I studied the town square through my riflescope. Another sundown meant another round of hell-raising, children without parents singing for the end of the world. Thing was, now I could hear the song too, and I knew none of them really understood the lyrics.

My ankle burned like someone was holding a lighter to it but the swelling had started to go down. That bite might have killed me under normal circumstances, but it was clear the snakes had a use for me. Fever burned up the back of my neck and I fell asleep there in the chair by the theater window, wondering if I was going to have to kill all my friends sometime soon.

I dreamed of stars and snakes, coiling and cold and reaching. They lashed around the earth, plucking it neatly from orbit and giving it a rough squeeze. Snakes beyond count, but lording over them all a giant reptilian face with supernova eyes. I realized that all those snakes were actually tentacles growing from that face. Our new gods were really just one great hungry god, and when he arrived we wouldn't die, we'd never have existed at all. The world screamed in the thing's grip and the voices sounded like my friends, my Mom and Dad, like Jacy and Duane and all the other flickering black and white denizens of small town Texas. The god squeezed harder and I could feel the breath leaving my lungs in a rush. Then it whispered its name to me and I woke up screaming and choking on the floor of the movie theater.

Through the window I could hear the voices of all those snakes with wonderful clarity, and I understood their intentions. They didn't want the world to end any more than I did. The rattlesnake song was a plea for help. The rituals they'd taught my friends weren't meant to summon a god; they were intended to keep us hidden, to cast a shadow over the world so that those horrible burning eyes couldn't see us. Dean and Stacey and all the rest thought they were bringing on the end of the world, but their rituals were actually the only things keeping their dark god at arm's length.

They were acolytes, wearing the skins of their god. But I'd been chosen the rattlesnake's prophet, and I wasn't ready for that god to walk our earth just yet.

I leaned my rifle in the corner, walked downstairs, and joined my friends in a circle, our fingers twined together and hands raised up, and we danced, spinning and writhing and lifting up our voices in prayer. Time began to wind more slowly around us and the roof of creation shuddered overheard, but did not collapse. Angry colors spilled from one horizon to another like rivulets from an overturned paint can, but we continued to dance, and laugh, and celebrate what remained of our youth.

The movie never gets old.

Most nights we take our seats in the old movie house and settle in for the death of Sam the Lion for the umpteenth time. We hate Jacy and we love her, and we root for Sonny to make better choices.

Gray threads crept into my hair long years ago and I have more in common with Sam the Lion these days than I do with all those celluloid teenagers and their desperate need to break away from their small lives. I'm okay here. It's my place. And besides, where else would I go?

The others are like my children now, and I feel their pain acutely. They are acolytes in full, with little remaining of the people they used to be, and they ache for the coming of their god. If they knew the ways I work against them, they'd kill me for sure, but I quietly resist and swallow the guilt of all the misery I'm causing them. The movie seems to be the only thing that brings them calm, so we gather together in the dark and we watch.

The movie plays every night, the refrigerators stay full of ice-cold Dr. Pepper, and the popcorn is always hot and buttery. I don't know if my rituals have frozen us in time or if the rattlesnakes have found a way to provide for us, but our tired town continues to lumber on, desperate to die but unable to rest just yet. Sometimes I wonder what's happening in the rest of the world, but it's a useless daydream. This place is our reality. These are our routines. Wanting more is just a shortcut to unhappiness.

When the movie ends, my children drift back to their warm holes and hovels, and I pull a blanket over me and sleep there in the theater seat. I dream about burning universes, about small towns full of dead teenagers, and of course the angry colors in the sky. They're always with me, asleep or awake, and they're hungry for this place.

Every morning when I wake, I look out the window to make sure the world is still there, and I give thanks. One night, I know, I'll go to sleep and never wake up.

I'm terrified of what'll happen to all of us then.

Josh Rountree's short fiction has appeared in numerous magazines and anthologies, including Realms of Fantasy, Daily Science Fiction, and Polyphony 6. His work has received honorable mention in both The Year's Best Fantasy & Horror and The Year's Best Science Fiction. A collection of his rock and roll themed short fiction, Can't Buy Me Faded Love, was published by Wheatland Press. For more info, check out his website at www.joshrountree.com.

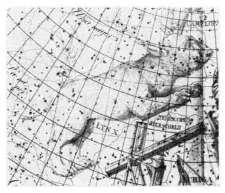

CATCH A FALLING STAR

STEPHANIE GILDART

The star fell from the sky, and Dena chased after it.

Same as she'd done ever since she witnessed her first falling star as a six-year-old. If you caught one of the Asteriae that came streaking downward toward the soil and released it back into the sky, it would grant you a boon. The boon didn't matter then. Dena and all the other children just needed an excuse to run around camp in the twilight, shouting and chasing and dreaming.

The star fell from the sky, and Dena chased after it.

Same as she'd done whenever she had the chance, since the night she realized Githis's right eye had never returned to its place in the sky. Or, rather, the star that represented the owl's eye in the constellation had winked out. Githis, the God of Storytellers, probably still had both of his eyes.

The star fell from the sky, and Dena chased after it.

Same as she'd done every night since her latest teacher had written her off as a lost cause and told her she'd be better off pursuing a career in something simple that involved no magic. How could she return home after this failure?

She couldn't. Not like this.

The star fell from the sky, and Dena chased after it.

Because she had to. Because, now, she needed a boon. Because, now, there were so few stars left to chase. Because Githis's right eye was the first star she'd noticed vanish, but it was far from the last.

The curve of tonight's star glowed brighter, felt closer. She left the trader's road with its deep wheel ruts, plunging in between trees with sparse undergrowth.

After four nights traveling on foot, she was low on food supplies. Tomorrow, she'd have to find a generous farmer who might be willing to spare a couple of meals or a town to stop in where she could exchange labor for food. She didn't have any money left. Her father would be all the more disappointed if he knew—a merchant's daughter who hadn't budgeted for her journey?

Shame.

Even more of a shame than being utterly incapable of any magic.

Her breath started coming up short, her muscles aching, so Dena slowed her pace. She rested one hand against the rough trunk of a tree as she passed by, pushed off of it, and kept walking forward at least. Every part of her pulsed with that steady beat of forward-moving Time.

Hitched breaths slowed her down more, and her vision blurred. She wasn't going to start crying alone in the woods. She wasn't giving up. This *wasn't* a fool's errand.

The whole reason her parents believed she had a penchant for magic was how she could hear the stars whispering, the voice of the asteriae. Like all nymphs, the asteriae spoke quietly to mages with an affinity for their elements—Light and Dark. Light was magic of creation, healing, and protection. Dark was magic of transformation, illusion, and amplification. Light and Dark magic together were the most complex magics, the most versatile, though not necessarily the most powerful. Her parents had been sure she only needed to find her niche, and then her magic would come.

Only, maybe her niche was *just* hearing the stars whisper. Nothing else magical ever worked for Dena.

She shoved those thoughts far away from her. It didn't matter if this was all foolish, if she was a lost cause. She had to try something, to believe something, even if all she had left to believe in was the existence of one foot to place in front of the other.

She sniffled away the dampness in her nose, blinked back the tears. Her vision cleared, and the rush of her pulse in her ears softened until she could hear the gentle breeze rustling through the forest canopy.

Then she heard a frenzied snapping up ahead somewhere, a struggling sort of sound. Then the shape of words.

"Let me go, let me go, let me go!"

Creeping forward, Dena kept close to a tree and tried to get a look at whatever might be out there, mindful of the sound her feet made, until she caught sight of the thing.

A shaggy wolf the color of midnight shadows had pinned down what looked to be an orange tabby cat with a set of rusty red wings twisted out behind it at odd angles, leaves and branches tangled between feathers.

A sharp icicle of fear plunged into Dena's heart. She knew the wolf wasn't a natural beast of the forest. The paralyzing fear came from it. It was a construct of the dark God of Fear, Krioch. Kriochin like this thrived on fear, terror, pain, suffering, and unnatural death. Twice in her life, her father's caravans had come across a kriochin. Both times, it took all the best fighters in the caravan to drive it back it. Both times, they'd lost at least one of their own.

The smart thing to do would be to leave the cat thing to the kriochin and travel straight home with her failure hanging around her neck like a noose.

Dena was not currently in the business of doing smart things.

She grabbed hold of the eating knife she wore at her belt—her best excuse for a weapon—drew it out, and charged out of her hiding place with a scream that came from every pain and disappointment she'd suffered trying to make her magic work. If she died, she died doing something brave and foolish.

Her sudden appearance startled the kriochin. It shifted its stance. The cat went squirming out from beneath the kriochin in a flash of fluttering wings and pedaling paws. All of the sudden it was up on Dena's shoulder, light as a pleasant summer breeze.

"Run away, now, human thing!" it shouted.

Maybe she didn't have any master fighting skills, but she knew how to run thanks to all those nights trying to chase the path of every falling star in the sky. She veered off to her left and plunged between the trees, away from the startled kriochin.

The kriochin howled in protest. Fear quickened Dena's breath more than the running did.

"Turn half-right. I saw a stream with a cave on the other side. The kriochin smells fear, but hope will mask all your fears. You did something incredibly brave. Hope, human thing, hope!"

The best hope she had was in following the winged cat's directions, so she did. Its warmth on her shoulders went to war against the chill in her heart, until she heard the babbling stream. Dena hastened her steps, splashed across, and dove into the cave mouth.

Dena usually associated darkness with fear, but in the shadows of the cave, bathed in warm hope, she found comfort. More like the darkness that made space for the asteriae to shine, the darkness that came with a quiet peaceful night's sleep. Less a shadowed villain's den.

The winged cat had gone still around her shoulders. It made no sound, spoke no further. Dena crouched in the shadows, eyes closed, concentrating on the warmth.

What did she have to hope for? Another night, another chance to chase stars?

An opportunity to ask this curious creature what it was?

These were small hopes, but hope and fear alike only needed small footholds. Soon the kriochin gave a snarl and splashed across the stream, so close. Fear tried to come icing through her veins again, but the winged cat dug its claws into her shoulders and gave a small little hiss, barely louder than the water burbling on its way.

Hope, hope, hope. Dena dove into her hopes, her memories, long days and starry nights on the road with her parents accompanying merchant caravans. She'd had simple hopes, then—the hope of seeing something exciting in the next town. The hope an old friend would still be living in the same place when they came back.

The kriochin snarled and snuffled and sought, claws scraping against stone near the cave mouth. Dena *hoped*.

When her parents sent her to study in the city, she'd had hope, too. Hope that her teachers would help her unlock her true potential. Hope that the whispers she heard really were asteriae, not a sign of some illness of the mind. Fear was so deeply entwined with these newer hopes, though. The chill rose in her, along with the memory of her failure and expulsion.

The kriochin stopped at the cave mouth. The winged cat nipped at Dena's ear.

The only thing that made any sense was the faint impossible hope that maybe she could catch one of the asteriae as they fell. Maybe one would grant her a boon. If she gave into fear and died here, that hope would die with her. Every chance gone.

No one would be surprised. Dena's whole existence was so small. No one would miss her.

Except for the winged cat she'd saved, which the kriochin would have eaten.

Dena bit down on her own lip, closed her eyes, and imagined the sky full of stars, the constellations she'd grown up loving before they'd begun vanishing.

The warmth swelled in her yet again.

The kriochin took a few shuffling steps before moving on. It didn't even bother to stick its head into the cave mouth. Without fear, it couldn't track them.

Still, they waited until the silence was only broken by the sound of wind rustling through tree branches, until common night creatures began to call out again, no longer hiding from the beast.

Only then did the winged cat retract its claws from Dena's shoulder. As the warm hope dimmed, Dena felt worry surge up again.

"Your wings," she said softly. "I've never... I don't know a lot about birds, but should I try to...."

"Get the branches and debris out of them?" the winged cat finished for her, leaping down to the cave floor. It emitted a very faint glow, enough that Dena could see about five feet around her now. "I'd appreciate that, human thing."

"My name is Dena." She shifted a bit so she'd be more comfortable on the stone, then reached out and started on the first branch. "What's yours?"

The cat fidgeted under her fingers, but where a common house cat might have started fighting, the winged cat's muscles only tensed slightly as it fought to stay still.

"My name is...." It trailed off.

Dena stopped short of pulling on the twig she was grasping. "Did I hurt you?"

"No, no. I... don't remember. That's strange. I've been called by my name every day of my life. I'm sure of it."

"I've heard when kriochin draw blood, they can also draw out fond memories," Dena offered. "Maybe it took your name."

"Then I'll have to hunt it down and get my name back."

Now the winged cat did spring out from beneath Dena's hands and leap toward the mouth of the cave. She had to hop to her feet and scramble after it, grabbing it the way she would have handled a wayward kitten—by the scruff of fur at the back of its neck.

"Not in the shape you're in, you won't," Dena objected.

"If it gets too far away, I won't be able to track it down. I'll lose my name forever!" Little clawed paws slashed out, and cat wings fluttered, but Dena held tight.

"You'll lose your life forever if we don't at least see to it you can fly properly," Dena retorted. "Come on. Settle down. Let's try to piece together what happened."

The winged cat struggled surprisingly gracelessly for a moment longer, then gave up and hung limp in her firm grip. Dena settled back onto the cavern floor, this time holding her companion more closely in her lap.

As Dena carefully worked the debris out of the cat's wings and smoothed its feathers, she grew curious. She'd found this creature while she was out chasing down the path of an actual falling star. The creature glowed and inspired hope in a human. The creature had attracted one of the fear god's own spawn.

But was this enough evidence to draw the conclusion it was an asteria?

She wanted it and hoped it and wished it. Because if it was an asteria, and if she helped it recover its identity from the kriochin, wouldn't it grant her the boon she so desired?

"If you can't remember your name, can I call you Ris?" Dena asked. "After Oris."

"The God of Hope." The winged cat bobbed its head in assent. "I could accept that name, for a little while."

"Ris, then. What do you remember?"

Ris, thusly named, leaned a little bit into Dena's hand as she smoothed the feathers of its now-folded wings. She was glad to find no signs of broken bones or more permanent physical damage, especially considering the kriochin's sharp teeth.

"I remember... flying. Catching Nuenda's winds and riding them upward. Folding in my wings and diving."

"Alone?"

Ris closed its eyes tightly, its face scrunching up as it thought harder about what it had been doing. "No. There were others like me playing together. There were... three kriochin! And three of us!"

Ris sprang up and flared its wings wide open, turning blindingly bright. Dena flinched away and covered up her eyes reflexively.

"My friends! They took my friends, and they took my name. I can't just stay here, human thing Dena. I have to save them."

"But, with what?" Dena asked, getting to her feet. This time, when she reached out to try and snag Ris, spots filled her vision, and she missed the catch. Ris was nimble, nimbler still with its wings put more or less back in order.

"I have claws. And hope. And determination."

"I'd feel better if we had knowledge," Dena replied. "Hope alone can only go so far."

"Then let's chase the kriochin down, so we know where they are, and we can save my friends!" Ris went bounding out of the cavern, a glowing streak of light leading her along the bank of the stream they'd crossed.

Dena sighed, then chased after it.

When she finally caught up to Ris, it had stopped glowing quite as brightly. It was perched on the branch of a tree at the top of a hill, the forest falling gradually away ahead of them. Tucked there in the valley, a strange black stone tower stood tall and imposing, solitary, strange. Ris turned its dark blue eyes toward her, blinked once, then its light faded out entirely.

"It went in there," Ris said softly. "The kriochin that caught me. I bet the other two are already inside."

"And I bet that's a mage's tower," Dena said.

"How can you tell?"

"My parents wanted me to be a mage, so I know. The best, most powerful who utilize the magic of Light and Dark do their work close to the sky, far from populated areas, especially if they're brewing potions or enchanting things."

She closed her eyes, thinking about how good it felt to lay on the roof of a barn and bask in the starlit glow, listening to the harmonies of Light and Dark, just that little bit closer to the sky. No wonder mages built towers.

"It's different for the Etheran-touched who work with fire and water and the like, or the Dream-touched, and much different for the After-touched. But the Light and Dark are drawn toward the stars."

Ris snorted. "I don't know what that has to do with me or my friends. We fly, and we play. Why would a mage send kriochin to capture us?"

"Why would a mage work with kriochin at all?" Dena replied. "No ethical mage would, at least."

Everything she'd been studying—and failing at—rattled around in her mind. Maybe she couldn't figure out how to grasp the magic and weave it into a spell, but she understood the theories. Working with kriochin meant working closely with fear, and while fear was as necessary to life as hope, all things were meant to be in balance, in correct proportion.

She tilted her head to one side in thought, then looked at Ris again.

The Dark. The kriochin. Fear.

The Light. The asteriae. Hope.

Balance.

"Too much thinking, not enough rescuing," Ris declared, coiling its muscles, ready to spring.

This time Dena was fast enough to grab Ris by the ruff of its neck again, and she turned her face from its fluttering furious wings.

"Not until we have a plan," Dena said firmly. "If it is a mage's tower, it might have protection spells woven somewhere around it. We have to make some kind of hole, so we can slip in unnoticed. Okay?"

Ris stilled. Then it seemed to phase straight through Dena's hand. One second she was grasping solid fur, the next she felt warmth like sunlight slipping straight through her fingers, and Ris was off, flying away. Dena had to spring to her feet to keep up.

She was wrong. She had to be wrong. She'd been wrong, unsuccessful, failing at so many things for so long that every time her feet pounded into the ground, she felt the word wrong resonate through her bones along with the impact. Wrong. Wrong. Wrong.

But, she could also smell the telltale smoke of a hearth fire from the tower, feel the cool night air against her skin. Ris was ahead of her, partly flying, partly leaping to bounce off of tree trunks and branches as they descended. Right or wrong, it was real. Dena was here, not dreaming.

And if she was right, and if Ris was an asteria....

Ris alighted upon a branch, coming to a sudden stop that snapped Dena out of those thoughts. She did her best to stop her downhill run without falling flat on her face, arms whirlwinding gracelessly.

"There!" Ris declared—voice somehow both soft and insistent.

A rope with a series of intricate knots hung between two branches ahead, just high enough that most people would pass beneath it without noticing it was anything other than part of a tree. But Dena recognized those knots.

It wasn't exactly the most common strategy for setting up a protection, but some mages took the idea of weaving magic a little more literally. They found the motion of tying knots or working a loom or other textile crafts to be the easiest way to channel their magical intent into reality. Dena had tied an awful lot of knots working under that principle.

It didn't work for her.

"I'll tear it down, yes?" Ris asked, spreading its wings, ready to fly up and do exactly that.

"No," Dena said quickly, before Ris could leap up into the tree. "If you tear it down, or cut it, or try to undo the wrong knots, it will trigger the warning spell just the same as walking beneath it would. Sometimes there's some kind of dangerous magic woven in that can cause harm to someone tampering with it, too. Can you help me climb up there? Point out branches that could hold me?"

Dena had climbed plenty of trees in her childhood. She didn't need Ris's help, technically, but Ris was acting so impulsively that she wanted to give it something to focus on.

It worked.

Ris patiently flutter-hopped up to one of the branches, low enough for Dena to grab hold of. "Start here."

Ris was a good guide, too, pointing out handholds and footholds Dena might not have noticed herself, right up until they were high enough for Dena to touch the knotted rope.

The rope had a sense of age to it, color faded from exposure to rain and sunlight, grime encrusted around the intricate knots. But this close up, Dena could make out the familiar patterns. Here was one that meant warning, then beacon, summoning…. All together, the knots told of a spell designed to send a warning to the tower and call forth its guardians.

She had to assume the guardians were the kriochin.

If she had magic of her own, she could dispel the mage's weaving with precisely-placed magical pressure. But she couldn't draw on the Dark in the night and its whispers of endings and Afters to make a slicing shadow blade that would sever both the rope and the magic it contained. She couldn't draw on the Light in the stars and moon and its song of creation and pulse of Time to create a silver-bright flame that would burn away at the magic but leave everything else around it exactly the same.

She had to settle for doing this the hardest way, by the strength of her hand and the knowledge in her mind.

Ris perched on a branch above her. Its tail swished, brushing the top of her head. "What are you thinking?"

"I only have one chance to do this right," she replied.

"Then do it, and be done," Ris advised.

Dena pressed her lips together and drew the knife from her belt. Either she did this, and it succeeded, or it failed. She knew where she needed to cut, if everything she'd learned about magic was true enough. Waiting any longer wouldn't change that outcome.

First, she sliced her knife across the trunk of the tree, carving into it deep enough to draw out sap. The bespelled rope was familiar with the tree—familiar not in an intelligent, sentient way, but in the way a rock leaves an impression in the earth when moved from its place. Unfamiliar things set the warning spell off, but the swaying of the branches around it wouldn't. Theoretically, the tree sap would keep the knife from setting the warning off, too.

She edged out on the branch, careful not to lean too far or swing her leg beneath the rope. Once she was out far enough, she chose the linking knot, the one where she felt almost certain she could cut into the spell without setting it off.

Then, slowly, carefully, she began to work.

"Keep watch, Ris," she said as she moved her knife back and forth across the knot, plucking away at it one filament at a time. "If anyone's coming, let me know. It'll take me longer to get out of this tree than you, after all."

Ris bobbed its head once in reply, focusing its attention around them. Its tail twitched rapidly, impatient.

Dena kept working at the rope. It would be easier if she could reach up and hold the knot to stabilize it while she carved against it. She grabbed some of the leaves, crushed them between her fingers, glad to feel they had some juice to them. Then she reached up to touch the rope. She hesitated only long enough to be sure the forest remained silent around them before she went back at it, faster now that she held the fraying knot in her grip.

The knot soon came apart, though the rope stayed in place, Dena swore she felt a tingling sensation run through her fingers and up her arms, magic dispersing. It was a complex enough knot, physically, that the rope probably wouldn't come loose around it unless she really pulled at it.

"Done," she said, relieved. "Now—"

Ris leapt from the branch and soared ahead toward the tower. "To the rescue!"

Ris's pronouncement wasn't loud, but it came with sharp exhilaration, piercingly insistent. When it passed beyond the rope, Dena felt no tremor of magic in the air, heard no alarms, saw nothing even remotely like a warning alarm spell getting tripped. She let out a sigh of relief and started down the tree as quickly as her arms and feet could safely guide her.

"Ris, wait up!" she called back with the same soft urgency.

Maybe they had a chance here. Maybe it would work out in their favor. Maybe, then, she would earn the asteria's favor, and—

The shadow sprang, so perfectly blended in with the nighttime gloom that neither had enough time to react. It oozed out from between the trees and solidified into that horrifying wolf-but-not form and pounced on Ris all in one motion.

Ris yelped, pinned to the ground once more.

Another shadow came coiling out from between the branches and draped around Dena's shoulders, then around her torso—a massive snake-shaped kriochin enfolding her with a hiss.

"Well, well, well," it said. "Little frightened rabbits for our master. Maybe she will let us eat you."

Dena's feet were lifted up off the ground, her body hefted up by the muscles of the coiled snake, her breath squeezed out, but she still managed one word.

"How?"

The snake kriochin chuckled as it began to undulate toward the mage's tower, and the wolf kriochin with Ris held in its jaws matched pace.

"Oh, you disarmed the warning spell, true, but who needs a warning spell when so much fear hangs thick in the air around you? The little lightling fears for its friends. You fear so very much. You've already disappointed your parents, your teachers, everyone who has ever counted on you. And now you disappoint the very thing you think could save you. Only, it can't."

The kriochin's words were worse than the squeeze of its powerful muscles choking out the air within her. Worse than any venom it could have inflicted her with in a bite. Worse than teeth or claws.

All Dena ever did was disappoint and fail, and now she'd failed again.

Ris tried to form some kind of words, but the wolf kriochin shook it fiercely and no words managed to make it to Dena's ears.

In the depths of despair, she and Ris were brought in through the door of the mage's tower.

Some mage's towers had levels, floors of stone—sometimes enchanted with protective spells—between each level. The greatest secrets were kept high in the topmost part of the tower. But this mage's tower was entirely open inside, from the ground floor up to the top, with a spiral of stairs and level balconies running up the path of the stone walls. High, high above, beneath the rooftop and breathlessly impossible, dozens upon dozens of stars glittered, suspended and still in place.

Dena only noticed the cloaked mage standing in the center of the ground floor when she threw her hood back, turned, and started toward the approaching kriochin.

"So you found the one that escaped, then," she said, voice chilly.

The wolf kriochin crouched downward in a slanted bow, though its jaws stayed clamped tightly on Ris, not giving the creature even a little bit of wiggle room to escape.

The mage gave a hum and an approving nod, then turned her dark blue eyes toward the snake kriochin. She locked gazes with Dena only for a split-second.

"Why did you bring me a human child? What use do I have for that?" she asked.

"She was able to disarm your warning spell. I thought you might want to cast judgement upon her personally before I ate her."

The mage looked back at Dena then, more appraising now.

"And why, exactly, did you disarm my spell? Who taught you? Who sent you?"

Dena felt the fear coiled around her seeping in through her skin. All was lost. There was no hope, but the tiny sparks of memory, the little flicker of the recollection of the hope Ris had given to her.

Even a small stray spark could start a fire. Traveling with her merchant father on the road had taught her that much. The wrong conditions could turn a shipment to ashes if evening fires weren't well-contained and watched closely.

She tried to focus on the spark of hope, what it meant, how it felt.

"I came because Ris's memory was stolen. Ris's friends were stolen away by Kriochin. I came because I am a star-chaser." Did the mage need to know Dena had only started chasing falling stars a few short days ago? No. The duration didn't matter. Dena pushed against that doubt. She was a star-chaser. "And now I see, you're capturing the stars."

The mage looked up then at the glittering spheres high above, lips curling in an odd nostalgic smile.

"My stars, my collection. I give them names, too. They feed my power and my pets, and my collection grows, day after day. Do you know why I collect them, child?"

"Steal them," Dena corrected. That spark was turning into burning embers in her chest.

"Collect. You can't steal something if it does not belong to anyone. You can't steal water from a lake that's meant for all. You can't steal the air we breathe. You can't steal stars."

"The asteriae belong to themselves! They are thinking, feeling beings!"

The mage waved her hand in the air dismissively and in the same gesture summoned forth a long wooden staff in one hand. Ropes and cords of different colors with various knots were bound around the staff, some wrapped tightly, others dangling loose. She began to wave it in the air, and a shimmer started to form around Ris. When the shimmering brushed against the wolf kriochin's muzzle, it loosened its grip and backed away quickly.

"If they thought, if they felt, they could escape. But they don't. They are mine. They know it. I have caught and collected them. I will them to stay." She didn't bother to look back at Dena again. "You may devour her, if you are hungry, serpent."

"My gratitude for your generosity, lady star collector," the serpent replied. It dropped Dena from its coils suddenly, but before she could so much as scramble away, it had opened its maw wide and clamped down over her legs, beginning to swallow her whole.

Panic at the thought of being eaten threw a fresh splash of cold fear over the hope Dena was clinging to desperately inside herself. But there was something in what the star thief had said that resonated with Dena.

If they had thought.

If they felt.

Instead of screaming or crying for mercy, she looked up at the flickering bright spheres.

"I remember when I was a child, my father told me the most dependable of all the constellations was Githis's Owl, ever gazing northward. Following its knowing beak on a clear night, travelers could find safe guidance toward their destinations. Are you up there, stars of Githis? Is this where you have vanished to? Travelers like my father miss your presence in the sky." A few of the spheres glowed a little more brightly, like they could hear her.

Was she imagining the way Ris turned toward her?

"My mother once told me she believed all falling stars really only fell because they wanted to hear children's stories about wishes granted. They wanted to lead the chase through the night, a chase that would inspire hopeful imaginations and leave behind fond memories, whether or not the children caught the asteriae. Have any of you ever led that game of Catch the Stars? I've chased you many, many times throughout my life."

More of the glowing spheres brightened.

The snake Kriochin started to swallow more quickly, but Dena locked eyes with Ris now. She knew her friend was looking toward her.

"When one among you lost its name, forgot what it was, still it was strong enough to remember to inspire a lonely, lost girl to hope in the face of darkness. She named it Ris, for the God of Hope, and they traveled together, hoping to save its other friends. Even not knowing parts of itself, it stayed true to its glowing warm heart. It hoped and it led her forward. Please, Ris, lead now. Remember yourself. She can't hold you. You are a force of nature. You are an asteria."

The snake kriochin had nearly finished swallowing her, but before its mouth closed over her eyes, she saw Ris find its feet.

As Ris stood, it also grew. The wolf kriochin lunged forward, but instead of tackling a small cat, now it was dealing with a great glowing lion of a thing with an aurora of a mane that rippled in green, violet, blue, and pink.

Darkness swallowed Dena, but not for long. Even through the fear-thick hide of the snake kriochin, she could hear Ris's roar like a lion, and the shattering of glass. Hope burned so bright within her that she pushed with her arms, with her legs, with the sheer willpower of it. Whether she clawed her way out of the fear creature's belly or Ris cut into the scaly hide, it didn't matter.

One moment she was in darkness.

The next, she was surrounded by swirling lights.

The mage, the star thief, screamed. The kriochin keened and faded back into the shadows. The stone of the tower cracked with the sheer magical force of a hundred asteriae remembering what they were and yearning to return to the sky.

"Grab on!"

Dena heeded Ris's call, reaching out to grab hold of its mane. She swung herself up onto the back of the star-lion as it spread its bright shimmering wings and launched itself skyward.

As long as Dena had chased stars, she'd never dreamed of pursuing them through the sky, but there she was, following in the wake of the freed asteriae, up and up into the Dark's firmament. The asteriae scattered in all directions as they rose higher, returning to their places or finding new ones to call home.

The Dark, Dena thought as she stared around her, was not a vast cold place of fear. The stars filled it with possibilities as limitless as her own future.

"A human thing can't live with us," Ris rumbled. Its voice sounded different, deeper, more sure. "Where can I take you, my star chaser?"

"Home," she said without thinking.

Home, she'd been so afraid to return to. Home, where her mother and father had told her stories of the stars and laughed as she and other children chased after them. Home, where she was a disappointment, a failure at magic. Home, where she might be accepted despite all that. And even if she weren't accepted, she could do so much with her knowledge even if she had no magic.

They flew through the night, until Ris dipped downward in a gentle spiral, descending toward a merchant caravan's fires. Dena could recognize her father's banner flying above the wagons in the dim light.

Did she climb off of Ris, or was she just... suddenly on her feet and running down the road toward the firelight?

Either way, it didn't matter. She knew the shape of her father standing watch in the early morning. His worried stance, hand hovering close to the hilt of his sword, shifted open the moment he recognized her, and he held his arms open to catch her up in a hug.

"Dena, I've been so worried," he said. He lifted her feet up from the ground and spun with her, like she was still a small child. When she came down again, she was laughing.

"Look, before the sun rises," she said, pointing up at the sky. "Did you see?"

As she followed the line of her own hand, she noticed the light glint off of a golden ring now wrapped around her index finger. It hadn't been there before.

The ring is my gift to you, Ris whispered in her thoughts. *Proof you are friend of the asteriae.*

She leaned into her father, and together they watched as each star flickered out and the sun rose above them, the dawn of a new day. When night fell, there would be more stars to chase, and by day, more ways she could use her knowledge to make the world better. With all the stars to guide her, even if she failed, she could find her way forward again.

Stephanie Gildart has been writing fantasy and science fiction for as long as she can remember. Growing up near Seattle, she checked out so many books that she memorized her library card number. She received her MFA from the Simmons University Center for the Study of Children's Literature in Boston. When she isn't writing or teaching middle schoolers, she loves to crochet amigurumi dolls of her favorite fictional characters, play tabletop games, and sing. She lives in the Bay Area with her dogs Fox and Lilly, who remind her to enjoy a nice walk outside every day (as long as it isn't raining). Follow her on twitter @stephgildart.

VENUS & THE MILKY WAY

RHEA ROSE

I crept down the boutique hotel's stairs like I did every night when I stayed in the city of Amsterdam. This was a special trip, and I wouldn't be back anytime soon. I needed to see the painting on display in the lobby, one last time. Every night, I promised myself I wouldn't go to the lobby to stare at the picture. But I did. The painting haunted me. Whenever I stayed at the hotel I thought of that painting. When I returned home and lay safely tucked into my bed, blinds shut tighter than they were designed to be shut in order to keep out the ever-present intrusion of the street lights that bled through every reinforcement no matter what, light that seeped through the cracks between my very worn blackout curtains, I thought of her: the statue of the woman in the painting. Whenever I found myself in Amsterdam, I stayed in this hotel, just so I could see the painting.

Even though no one sat at the front desk of the hotel, no one checked in at this time, the lights still shone brightly, luminescent soldiers of modernity illuminating every small space, so no one could hide in any corner without being revealed to the security cameras. I'd paused for a moment to investigate the tiny black and white screen of a security TV to make sure no one wandered, zombie-like, unable to sleep; it appeared that no one did. In this city of millions, it seemed as if no one existed at this time of night in any capacity, walking on the street, moving in the back lanes, or anywhere.

I made my lonely journey across the lobby's front floor. Through the large, bayed front window, and beyond, the street outside led to one of the many small, ancient bridges that spanned the canal's black and liquid contents full of morphed reflections that stretched then blobbed on the water's surface caused by the glow of street lamps, very much like a Van Gogh painting; farther on, under a starry red light, a woman sat on a stool in a window.

2 a.m.

Only those that descended the staircase on the other side of the hotel lobby might chance a glance at the painting. As I climbed those old narrow stairs, each one creaked a small song of protest. When I found my spot, I turned to look at the picture and the same old sensation of dreamy flight that it always caused, took hold of me. An oil painting of a version of the naked back of Venus de Milo. She stood in the darkest night on a hill overlooking an unidentifiable land, her white marble skin lit only by the Milky Way. I swear I heard the soft hissing twinkle in those stars.

I stared and fought the threat of sleep. Steady, armless, and with long hair to the middle of her back, she looked as if she was about to fly; the Doric style pillar on which she stood tilted and created the sensation of vertigo, a tipping forward that never quite lost its balance, but if it ever did, she would fall down the hill, for now she only forever-threatened to topple head over plinth into that black village below, her stars, her Milky Way watched, a dark passage of vigilance.

I was her, and she was me.

The hotel creaked and groaned. It smelled like old smoke and fruity cigarettes, oranges and cinnamon. I held the wooden stair banister as I stalked the painting with my eyes, my feet trying to find the best step to stand on, one up, one down, forever standing behind her beautiful back, wishing to stand beside her to share the view, but while she forever stared down at the lights in the village below, I could not take my eyes off the starlight painted above her. I'd never seen the Milky Way like this; I'd never seen the Milky Way at all, except in pictures and paintings.

In Amsterdam, no one ever saw the deep stars.

I stood for an hour, I think, and finally I started to feel sleepy. I had the next day to myself, so I wasn't concerned about sleeping in, or getting enough rest. I planned to take a few of the flight attendants on a tour of the red-light district tomorrow; many had never walked it. But I knew from experience that they'd be falling out of bed closer to noon than morning. As I stared, transfixed on Venus' night sky, wishing to fly into and across it, I noticed that her head had changed position. I closed my eyes, rubbed them, opened, and blinked. Yes! She had moved! Her white marbled profile, never visible before, now stood out in contrast against the black canvas.

I decided I needed to get some sleep and left my perch. I reached into my flight jacket, which I'd tossed on over my pajamas, and dug around in a pocket for one of my melatonin sleeping pills. I'd already popped a couple of them earlier, but nothing made me feel tired. The bottle suggested a limit of three.

Halfway across the cool black and white checkered lobby floor, I caught movement on the street. A man hovered outside the display glass window of the woman seated within, on a stool. Her red light on. She must have pressed a button somewhere because in a moment I saw him try the nearly invisible door next to the window. He opened it and went inside. I stood in the lobby to watch the drama of the moment.

Her light went out.

It didn't take long for the red light to come back on and her gentleman visitor to vacate the premises. She sat back in the window but with her back to me. And that struck me as weird. And though the window light shone provocatively on her butt and shoulders, at the angle she sat it looked as if her arms were missing. I watched this illusion for a few seconds and then she turned her head ever so slightly in such a way that her profile became visible. Stunned by the coincidence of her look to that of Venus in the painting, my mind went blank. The next thing I knew, I'd headed out the door, to the bridge, across the canal, and into the woman's shop.

Or I tried to.

The door resisted, locked. I looked up. The red light still on. Then I heard a voice, disembodied, Dutch, like German only much softer. I spoke back, but in English. "Your light is on."

"I only take men customers," she said in English.

"I don't want sex," I said.

A long pause. "What then?" she asked me.

How to explain to this person-of-the-night that she possessed the same look, profile, sense of longing as the statue in the painting. I realized how ridiculous that would sound and turned to leave. I heard the click of the lock on her door.

Open.

I grabbed the handle, but not before I noticed the small drone that magically appeared in the alcove of the doorway. It lifted away from a part of the roofing tiles above her shop, came to life in a moment. Its yellow security eye scrutinized me. I entered the shop, and so did the drone.

The woman, still on her stool, locked inside her glass cage, wore a tight-fitting, strapless black dress, a pair of very worn out, black, strappy, platform shoes, and she smoked something long and metallic, a vape of sorts but unlike any I'd ever encountered. She spoke to me through the glass. "Put money on the table," she said, indicated a small marble topped table with her knitting-needle-like vape. I reached deep into my flight jacket and pulled out a fist full of dollars, euros. She seemed satisfied with this. The drone picked up the cash and dropped it into a small safe that opened in the floor. "What do you need from me?" she asked.

"The painting," I stuttered. "The one in the hotel lobby, across the street," I turned and pointed, "Are you the model for it?"

She grinned hard and continued biting on the thin smoking instrument, her lips very red, but her teeth were a soft yellow. Her hair white and curly like Marilyn Monroe's. "Perhaps," she said, teasingly. The drone hovered at my shoulder, just behind me.

"I'd like to buy it," I said.

"It's not for sale. One of the few things on this street not for sale," she said, smiling demurely. "Anything else?" she asked. I panicked, I knew that at any moment I'd hear the click of the lock on the door and be expected to step back out onto the street. My moment with Venus over. I didn't want to leave. And then she spoke, "She wants something."

"What? What does Venus want? Anything I have in my power to give. Anything."

"You think you're the first to want her?" she asked. I watched her in her glass cage, chewing on that metal stick, sucking on it for sustenance; suddenly I became Alice at the foot of the mushroom, talking up to the caterpillar. And everything seemed to me like an impossible riddle. "Tell me please. What does she want?" I asked, not sure what to expect.

"Isn't it obvious, Meisje?

"Not to me," I said, quietly.

"She wants to look up—"

"Up?"

"—to see the stars, to see the Milky Way above," she said, taking another deep inhalation of her smoke; then she used the long vape to point to the ceiling. "But she never can. Can she? She can never behold the universe, never look upon one of its greatest mysteries."

I stood stunned. I cried a little. "Are you—"

"Am I what? I am not the model for her."

"But your explanation—it's so deep—so, I don't know, connected."

"Well, then you know, don't you?" she said, coldly. "You know who I am."

I nodded, pretending to know the answer to that. I had no idea who she was. But she reminded me of someone I'd once loved and lost. Someone to whom I'd broken a promise wished upon a star. I got cold. I pushed my arms through the long sleeves of my military flight jacket. I looked for the drone, but didn't see it. Maybe it slept somewhere, the light of its yellow eye gone out. I wished I could sleep. It must've been four in the morning, still dark, but, even though the window in which she sat loomed large, the night sky wasn't visible between the district's lights.

A man passed the window, walking slowly, his hands in his pockets; he walked by two, three, four times. I sensed his impatience. My hostess straightened her back, pushed out her chest, crossed and uncrossed her legs, focused on the potential customer.

"Your light's out. What does he want? I paid my money, too," I said, reminding her of that fact, feeling annoyed at having lost her attention.

"Don't be like that. Remember, we are the same," she said.

I gave her my most confused look. Shook my head, negatively.

"No?" she asked. "She is me, and you are her. Didn't I hear you say that?" she asked, repeating my thoughts back to me, or had I said that aloud? "You've come, Meisje, to make amends. To repair a forgotten promise to an old love."

Then I heard the click. I looked up at her in the window, but she'd already cast her sight on the man waiting patiently, leaning against the post near the canal.

I left and went back to my room.

The next day, I went on my tour, showed the other flight crew around the district, careful not to draw any attention to the window across the street from my boutique hotel. Every moment I had the opportunity to glance at her spot, where she sat, night after night, I did. Only her high painted stool remained there, in its position. Of course, she didn't sit there all the time, especially during the day. I'm sure she went shopping like all of us. Went to visit her mother and did all the mundane things we all find necessary. I tried to remember what time she normally came to the window. To turn the red light on.

That night I went to look at the painting. I decided I'd take my chances and steal it. What did it matter? In the morning I'd be gone, on my way to the Mars colony for a three-year stint at the old base. The painting of Venus would be my best company, and if anyone at the hotel figured out who'd stolen it, well, there'd be nothing anyone could do. I plotted, borrowed tools from the hotel caretaker closet, in case the painting was bolted to the wall.

I waited till all the world slept except for me.

And while I lay on my bed, my flight bags packed for my three-year Martian tour of duty, I plotted how I'd get that picture off the wall and secret-ed into my gear; it was then that it came to me. An epiphany. The light came on in my head, and I realized what Venus wanted.

When 2 a.m. rolled around, I found myself back on that staircase, staring one last time at the painting. I'd convinced myself that hallucinations, induced by my lack of sleep, dream-walking, if you will, had caused me to see the profile of Venus. Now, I saw only the curve of her back and hips, the pillar and plinth of her forever-almost-fall and the call of the stars striped across her night sky. When I reached up to take the painting, I expected resistance, the kind I'd met when I tried to open the door across the street the night before. But of course, there was no resistance. The picture came away. Anyone could have taken it home, if they'd wanted. I stood for a moment holding it, looking down into the magic well of its call. I had it, and close-up it was larger in my hands than when it hung on the wall—and then, there it was, her profile, her lovely eye looking over her shoulder at me, as if any moment she'd shift on her plinth and turn to face me. I swear I saw that smile on her lips, the one she gave me in her shop. "I know what you want," I said to the painting. My voice sounded loud, even to myself. I looked up to see if my sound might have brought anyone, but no. I did see myself in a small security TV I'd never noticed before in the stairwell. I didn't care. When I looked back to the painting, Venus had returned to her position, facing forward, away from me looking down at the village, the stars above twinkling, and I heard them hiss their starlight at me.

Boldly, with the painting under my arm, I went to the lobby. I stopped at the window there and looked out. There was no one. I looked across the street, but she was gone from her glass cage. Her red light out. I waited, but she didn't return. I heard someone wandering inside the hotel, perhaps the caretaker. Maybe someone actually watched the security TVs at night, maybe they came to apprehend me. I took one quick glance across the street, but her dark window only reflected street light, and her red star gone quiet. Not even the yellow eye of the guard, the drone. I looked down at the painting and decided that if I left a few personal belongings behind, the painting could fit inside my suitcase, safely wrapped in soft things; it would survive the trip.

When I turned around to head back to my room, Venus stood there in the empty lobby, smoking her vape, dressed in her black dress, platform shoes, Marilyn's soft, white hair. Tonight, her lips were painted black. I put my free hand to my chest to calm my heart which threatened to beat beyond its capability. She stared at me. The caterpillar had climbed down from her perch. Feeling very busted, I shifted the painting and held it out to her. She didn't move, but assessed me, the situation, her winged eyes as objective as a drone's, then, ever so slightly shook her head, no. I took the painting back, re-tucked it under my arm. I expected the police to arrive at any moment.

"Keep it," she said.

I gave her my best look of surprise. "You won't tell?"

Then she laughed. I realized in the hard glare of the hotel lobby light that she was old. Much older than she'd looked in her glass cage. Still sexy, still desirable, but perhaps a grandmother. She'd had work done to her face, her eyes looked young, her mouth plump and her teeth now like white pearls.

"Have you looked at it?" she asked, in her softly accented English.

"It's burned into my mind," I answered.

"The artist."

That comment caught me off guard. I pulled the painting forward, flipped it over and looked for a signature. I found it. I looked at her. She sucked long and hard on her incredibly long sharp vape, now reminding me of a stiff hookah's hose. Then, incredibly, for the second time that night, a light went on in my mind, *she'd painted it.* Venus was the artist. "You?"

"You want me, but nothing is free, Meisje."

"How much?'

She came toward me. She came in very close. I saw her clearly then. The businesswoman. For an instant, I felt afraid.

"I know what you are," she said. I froze. For the moment, I was nothing more than a thief. What else did this mysterious woman know about me?

"I've met so many flight people over the years. Many."

Of course, that made sense, in her line of business, all the hotels, tourists, flight crews. Hundreds, possibly thousands.

Then she leaned in and whispered into my ear. "The highest price," she said. She spoke in Dutch, "Steek de sterren aan." Slowly, I shook my head, no. "I'm sorry," I said, "Can you tell me in English?"

"For Chrissake, put it in your translator on your ship," she said. Then she looked away because something caught her attention outside. A man prowling her window, across the canal. She looked at me. "Don't forget. A second chance," she said. She reached into her bag which I hadn't noticed and pulled out a small gadget. A phone, I thought, and I was right. She slid it awake and pushed her long-nailed finger to an app on its screen. The red light above her door went on. The man stopped there and pulled the door open. He went inside.

She looked to me one last time. "Tomorrow evening, late. I won't be working. You'll be leaving. I'll be watching," she said. Then she moved gracefully into my space and kissed me. Her warmth ignited something in me which I hadn't felt for so very long. Had I once known her? I came through here often. Had we connected? Always sleepless, always on duty, had I forgotten her somewhere along my travels?

She moved to the hotel's front door, unlocked it, and headed out into the night. I watched her for a while. The incessant lights of the street marked her passage, but at one point she stepped into a shadow, and only her white hair was left visible, like a softly glowing moon, and then she disappeared.

The next day, transport arrived and picked up the rest of my crew. It was an early morning launch; they fed us breakfast on the long drive to the port. My ship looked clean and sparkled even in the dull, polluted city light. Excited to get on board and put my painting up in my cabin, I stumbled my way through customs, wishing that I'd bothered to research how the legality of transporting Dutch art from Earth worked.

No one said anything about the painting.

Once launched and all systems go, I relaxed and allowed myself to look down on the city of Amsterdam. The farther we lifted away, the more the millions of pinpricks of light coalesced to become one large yellow glob of luminescence, and only then did I remember Venus' words.

I quickly moved to the translator and tried my best to speak them into the com system. I did something right, because the system came back and spoke the words more correctly to me in Dutch. "In English," I requested.

"Light up the stars."

I panicked. All at once, I understood.

In payment for the painting, Venus had asked me to light up the stars. And she knew I could do it. I feared I may have missed my opportunity. Quickly checked my flight instruments. Checked Amsterdam time. Counting on old, long held favors, I called my communications officer and engineer back from their break. They grumbled about our procedure, but I explained.

The stars are ours.

They belonged to her and her world as much as mine and finding them again was a calling—from the goddess.

With my small crew in place, I led the countdown to a baby-sized and very directed electromagnetic burst, a pulse calculated for a radius of five kilometers around the city that wouldn't affect the emergency systems or nearby hospitals. I wasn't too worried. They all had their own preventative measures for that kind of off-the-grid situation. The best Amsterdam time for complete darkness came at twenty-two hundred hours their time, and as luck would have it, high coronal activity in the atmosphere created a great cover for my very illegal maneuver.

If Venus watched tonight, and she said she would, she'd have a view of the Milky Way for two hours from anywhere in the city. Or for as long it took the technicians to squelch the activity. The pulse would knock every light and electronic gadget off its kilter. If she remembered to look up, she'd see the stars for the first and only time in her life.

Rhea Rose of Vancouver, Canada has published many short speculative fiction stories and poetry. She received honorable mentions in the (2014, 2010, 2007) Year's Best Horror anthologies, has twice made the preliminaries for the Nebula Award, and was three times an Aurora Award nominee for fiction and poetry. She is a teacher of creative writing, holds an MFA in creative writing from UBC, has and still does edit poetry and fiction; a long-ago Clarion grad, she has hosted and still participates in the Vancouver Science Fiction and Fantasy (VCon) writers' workshops. Her most recent stories and poems are included in Second Contacts, Art Song Lab, Clockwork Canada, Tesseracts 20 Compostela (Fall 2017), 49th Parallels Alternative Canadian Histories and Futures, 2018), and she is a stargazer, also an Indie writer with collections of her work to be found at Amazon and Smashwords. www.rheaerose.weebly. com (website), www.rhearose.com (blog), Twitter: @rheaerose1

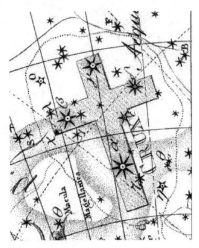

WHAT PRICE THE SKY?

MIKE BROTHERTON

"I won't waste any more of your time, Mr. Mayor. My clients want to buy your sky," Ms. Zhao said with the hint of a New York accent. "They want the sky that inspired genius, and they'll pay top dollar."

John Gonzalez paused mid-step and turned to look at her. In the yellow glow of the sodium lamp half a block behind them, it wasn't easy to make out her expression, but it was a serious one. "Buy our sky?"

"That's right," she said. "You have it exactly right."

Ms. Zhao had called him earlier that day, identified herself as a lawyer, and requested this unusual after-hours meeting. She said she represented interests that had a proposition for Springbranch. John had agreed to the late meeting, but joked that she could bring him a bottle of tequila for his trouble. She'd shown up at his house in an Auto just after dusk, her sharp suit making him feel underdressed in his t-shirt and jeans, but it was summer in Texas. She had handed him a bottle of tequila, even though it hadn't really been necessary, and asked if they could go for a walk. That had been odd, but this was getting odder.

"Our airspace?"

"No. Your sky, or at least your view of the sky."

"Well, we're using it," he joked. He did that when he was uncertain.

She didn't laugh, but she did crack a small smile. "Are you open to an offer?"

He gave it a moment's thought before he replied. "I'm open to anything that might benefit our town, but I really don't know how we can literally sell our sky, although your comment about inspiring genius indicates why someone wants to buy it."

She pulled her phone from her purse, tapped the screen a few times, and then put it away. "I've just sent you the proposal to review. Be warned that there is a non-disclosure agreement covering some particular details. Will you present this to your citizens in a timely manner?"

"Yes, I can do that. I would have anyway, without you making the trip. I'm sorry you went to the trouble."

"No trouble," she said. "My clients insisted I meet you in person to impress upon you that this is a serious offer. And besides, I wanted to see it for myself."

Ms. Zhao looked up, and then he did as well.

They had walked east through his neighborhood and were at the edge of town, which provided a relatively good view of the sky. He spotted Vega ahead, with Deneb and Altair below, forming the summer triangle. To the right, he made out the teacup of Sagittarius, and the Milky Way pouring up from there through Scorpio and the rest of the Zodiac. Both Jupiter and Mars hung nearby, farther south. Continuing to spin around slowly, the Big Dipper and the Little Dipper came into view as he faced north. A good dark sky, protected by the county lighting ordinance that supported the McDonald Observatory, not so many miles away. Like many in Springbranch, it was a matter of pride to know his way around the sky, at least a little bit.

"It's nice," she said.

"It is," he said, lowering his gaze and finding her face again.

She was looking up with a quizzical look, but he didn't know her well enough to know how to interpret that. Abruptly she got out her phone, its screen bright on her face. She whispered to it, then looked back at the sky. Frowning, she said, "Unfortunate. Ruined my night vision."

"It will come back."

But the Auto must have been waiting for her quite nearby, because it silently pulled up with its blistering headlights, and Ms. Zhao got inside. "Thank you for your time, Mr. Mayor. I will be in touch."

"Short visit," he said, as the electric vehicle moved away.

John remained, his neck crooked, considering the sky above Springbranch. It was a fine sky indeed, even from in town.

Then a mosquito bit him on the neck, so he walked home.

Back in his mostly mosquito-free, air-conditioned house, John picked up the bottle of tequila he'd been gifted. A sun design adorned the tall, clear bottle with the brand name Barrique. He hadn't heard of it before. He opened it and sniffed the dark liquid inside. Smelled like booze. He poured himself a glass to sip and tried it.

A bit different. John preferred Jose Cuervo, but this would suffice. Now fortified, he had some work to do to review Ms. Zhao's proposal.

First thing, however, he needed to remind himself of just what his cousin had said. He carried his tequila to the couch in front of the TV. "Find me that episode of Cosmos from last year, the one with the segment about Mary Jane."

A soothing beep acknowledged his request and a moment later John saw his slim cousin wearing a pale blue sundress sauntering down Elm Street. She had Texas-sized swaths of dark hair, no gray visible yet, wide-open eyes, and a contagious enthusiasm that made her a popular choice for interviews.

"I grew up here, in Springbranch, Texas. A lot of the other kids didn't think much of growing up in a small town. High school football was the big show, the Friday Night Lights, as they call them." She was now walking beside the football field, and through the magic of TV, night fell and the floods exploded over running and grunting players. "But those lights weren't the ones I preferred."

The camera panned up into a rapidly darkening sky, a bit different from the one he'd been looking at earlier. They'd gotten the details right, he had to admit, with fall constellations as you'd actually see them from Springbranch during football season, at least after the lights went out. They'd probably go out totally next year, as it was getting hard to field a team given the steady population decline.

And then she voiced over what he'd been searching for. "The richest billionaire living in New York City can't buy a sky like this, and it was gazing at this sky that led me to the insight that helped us to finally crack the puzzle of dark energy."

"Pause," he said. The twinkling stars on the TV stopped twinkling.

Their sky could indeed be said to have "inspired genius." That was indeed it, the thing that made the sky of Springbranch a commodity, at least to big city billionaires who surely hated being told they couldn't buy something.

"Okay," John muttered to himself, grabbing his tablet off the end table. Time to exercise that UT law degree. "Let's see how you think you can buy a sky, and exactly what you're offering."

He started reading, and continued long after his glass was empty, excited and concerned in equal measures.

A week passed before John felt that he fully understood the situation well enough to present the offer fairly with its pros and cons. He scheduled a town hall meeting.

The gymnasium was fuller than he'd seen it before, even fuller than the homecoming dance. They'd had to bring in chairs from the cafeteria to augment the bleachers. He knew nearly everyone in town, their faces if not their names or life stories, and he began to look for the people he knew were Springbranch's heartbeat. He spotted Katy Salinas, who waitressed at the Supper Club, and George Peterson, who ran the Overnight Inn, two of the people through whom most of the gossip ran. Julie Harris, also, the petite woman who owned the Coffee Jolt with the attached charging station. He'd talk to them in a day or two, if necessary. He also saw Father Marin, whom John regarded as the town's spiritual leader. Most of the crowd was scanning the summary handouts he'd prepared. Scanning very intently.

The gym was still warm after the sunny afternoon, as he'd expected, but this was an occasion to wear a suit. Feeling even warmer, John got up from his seat and went to the microphone that had been set up for him.

"Testing, testing," John said. Loud with no feedback, good.

"Hello, friends," he began. "We've been approached with an unusual proposition. I want to present it fairly to you, and hear what you have to say. This is a decision for the people of Springbranch to make. I can't make it for you. We have to make it together. It would forever change us, so let's give it some thought."

He waited for a beat, feeling like he'd provided a proper disclaimer. The truth was that he could present this proposal and advocate for one side or the other, but he himself was conflicted, and he really did want to know what people thought. He worried that he might be failing to display the leadership that a Mayor should, but he'd decided. This was a decision for the town to make together.

Many heads were still down in order to read the summary, but most looked up and gave him their attention.

"Here's what is on deck." John went on to describe the proposal, which he regarded as outrageous, but also checked out. For a very large sum of money to Springbranch itself, for "infrastructure or other community benefits," as well as to individual property owners, Ms. Zhao's unnamed clients would put the entire town under a dome. A very big dome. The dome would be covered in high-resolution cameras, practically telescopes, that would cover the dome like hair and collect a live feed of their sky. The money would be paid in installments and was dependent upon continued occupancy of Springbranch. After laying out some of the more important details, he opened the floor to questions.

There were those asking for more information.

"Will it rain inside?"

"In essence. There's a sprinkler system that would run between 2am and 3am, three days a week. We could modify that schedule if we like."

"Will it be climate-controlled?"

"Yes, and we can change the default offerings as we like."

"Will there be mosquitoes?"

"They're not guaranteeing anything about the mosquitoes, but I bet we can do a better job inside a dome."

"What about sunshine? And our yards and trees?"

"A mirror system will bring us something close to natural sunlight. We should be able to maintain our yards as we like, although getting rid of the extremes of summer and winter will cause some changes."

"Did you screw up the decimal points? I can't believe it's this much!"

"It's correct. And I verified with the escrow service. They have the funds already waiting for us."

There were those that were more suspicious, and John answered those with his best guesses.

"Why can't we take the money and leave?"

He sighed. "I think because then it won't be Springbranch's sky. They want our sky, so we have to be here without it."

"Isn't that kind of mean?"

"Perhaps."

"Why don't they save a lot of money, buy some scrub land, and get practically the same thing?" Pete Jones asked. He had a big ranch with less than desirable land.

"Same answer. Then it would not be Springbranch's sky. Not the sky that inspired Mary Jane Gonzalez to develop her astrophysics theory." Everyone knew all about their most famous citizen. The souvenir shop at the charging station was mostly books and postcards about her.

"Can we take vacations? Or go for walks outside the dome?"

"Yes, but only under the stipulations outlined. At least 300 days in Springbranch, of at least 20 hours a day."

"What's the catch?

"I think the catch is that we lose our sky."

"Is that all?"

"As far as I can tell."

There were those who made comments.

"This is a lot of money, and we'd be idiots not to take it."

"Did you get a load of the heat today? Living in a dome would be a huge improvement."

"We could be a tourist attraction and make even more money!"

"I'd miss the sky, wouldn't you?"

"What would Mary Jane think?"

"Mary Jane doesn't live here anymore."

Father Marin finally weighed in, as John hoped he would. Standing up, people quieted. Not everyone in town was Catholic, but many were, and he was respected. "This is a choice we face. The easy choice is money, to give up something we take for granted. But the earth and sky are the Creation itself, and we turn our back on either at the peril of our souls. Isn't this the very definition of selling out? If we would trade this for mere money, isn't that the start of a slippery slope? Isn't that the one thing we have that makes us Springbranch?"

These words echoed one side of John's thoughts, the ones he let out lying in bed waiting for sleep to come. He was glad someone was voicing them – someone should. They really did have a nice sky, and it seemed wrong that some rich people could just assume that they could take it because they had money, and the technology allowed it. But he could do so much for Springbranch! They could get all the streets paved. Get the drainages fixed. Reopen the library. Get a few more Autos for in town so that no one had to wait. Heck, in his secret heart he thought about a regular delivery of fresh fish and opening up a sushi restaurant, something he really did miss from his law school days in Austin.

An older woman in a wheelchair, Jane Chilton, John recalled, yelled out, "I got cancer! I need that money or I'm going to die!"

There was silence, then a smattering of applause. Then another person, a tall man in back, yelled, "We're giving up our sky. They're rich. Can't you get them to up their offer?"

That brought enthusiastic applause.

John suddenly realized that they were all rationalizing how much they needed the money, even though only a few likely had such desperate immediate health issues. Was having good sushi worth giving the rich people their sky? Probably not, he admitted to himself, but what about human lives? That was worth selling out, wasn't it?

The sushi would be a bonus.

"Thank you, all," John said as the hour lengthened into evening. "Please take the opportunity to enjoy the stars on your way home. It sounds like we may not have them much longer."

John closed the meeting with a promise that there would be a referendum the following week. He caught Father Marin's eye for a moment, a bit embarrassed, while everyone else around them chattered excitedly about how they would spend their windfall.

He had little doubt that they would sell out, and he wanted to sell out, too, even though he knew it would exact a price on them all.

John dreamed that he was chained to the mast in the crow's nest of an old-time sailing ship that violently rocked in a stormy sea. Cold water doused him. Wind howled. Below him on the deck were Jane Chilton and Father Marin, looking up to him to guide them to safety, but because of the storm clouds there were no stars to guide him, and he could see no land.

They yelled at him, urging him to do his job, to keep them safe.

He was chained, but somehow the ship's wheel was before him. He spun it clockwise, then counterclockwise, as giant waves threatened from different directions.

Lightning crashed, and in its flash, he saw a looming island with a large sea cave. He steered for it.

After a few frightful minutes they sailed inside. Inside the cave was pure blackness, although somehow the ship was still in light. Inside the cave was calm. Inside the cave was safety. But as he looked around in a panic, he realized there was no way out.

Waking, he gasped. His blankets were wrapped all around him and his body was sweaty. He rose to get a glass of water.

On the way back to bed, he grabbed his tablet. It was late in Springbranch, but not so late in Hawaii. He Zoomed Mary Jane. He really should have already, but he felt a bit embarrassed.

After only two rings, she answered. "Hola, John!"

Despite the relatively late hour, she looked perfectly put together, like always. He knew she didn't have her make-up artist like she did for TV appearances, but there was something about her that always looked good. Her eyes were warm and friendly, and her teeth a little whiter than most people's. It sometimes didn't seem fair that she should always look good and be so freaking smart, too. Maybe she was running a video filter, but he doubted it. That wasn't her style.

"Hola, Mary Jane. I have to talk to you about something."

"I know. You called me." She smiled. She was smart.

"Springbranch has had an offer." But he needed to be careful. "I can't tell you too much about it right now, okay? But I think talking to you might help me find our way through the pitfalls."

"Of course," she replied.

"Okay," he said. "You made our skies famous. Rich people want to buy them."

"Buy them?" She seemed honestly surprised. She was smart, but couldn't mind read.

"Yes. They want to build a dome over the town and intercept all the light. They're going to do something with it, because they want to put cameras on it, pipe it to the billionaires for their own houses and parks, I'd guess. New York at least. I'd guess also Dubai, Tokyo, all over. And it's sort of your fault."

"My fault?" Her expression suddenly shifted. "Oh. I get it. Sorry."

Of course she got it. Genius. "Well, don't be sorry. You have to do your thing. But, really, you made us sound like the best place since the invention of the taco truck, and while I'm not going to talk bad about Springbranch, it was a bit much."

"I see."

Okay. Time to move beyond his own insecurities. He had to assume some responsibility for Springbranch, even though he had left things up to a vote. John still wanted her advice. "They're really offering a lot of money. Do we sell our soul to the devil?"

She asked how much money.

He explained the deal.

"Mierda," she whispered. "You have to take that, right?"

"Probably," he agreed. "Jane Chilton has cancer, and she's not the only one with expensive health issues."

She said nothing, but she looked down and her lips tightened. After a moment, she said, "West Texas skies are dark, but they're not the best I've seen."

"They're not?" he asked, genuinely surprised. Springbranch's skies were really good. Inspiring even, right? He suddenly felt indignant. Where was better?"

"I get to go everywhere," she said. "Locally here, Mauna Kea, is totally awesome. It's probably the best in the northern hemisphere. But Chile blows it away."

"What's so special about Chile?"

"Everything." She paused for a moment and looked up, considering. "The Atacama desert is so dry. Humidity is less than ten percent year round, it almost never rains, and barely any plants grow. The air comes over the Pacific, so smooth. I've seen the green flash there, at sunset, three times. The Zodiacal light most nights. Orion upside down is great. The Magellanic Clouds, the Coal Sack. Alpha Centauri. Springbranch is great, but it isn't the best."

John felt a little bad about that. He'd never traveled the way she had, but he was Mayor of the best town with the best, darkest skies. Wasn't he? But Mary Jane was the expert. He had to listen to her.

"Okay," he said. "You know, we take this deal, we're going to have a little money, too, even earmarked for infrastructure. Do you think Chile would be willing to sell a few square miles of this barren desert where we could set up our own cameras?"

A smile grew across her face. "I bet they would. I know just the person to talk to."

"Thanks. I'll call you tomorrow and we can start talking with them."

"Sure, sounds good. Now go back to bed. Your eyes are bloodshot and frankly, you look exhausted. Maybe you can sleep now." She winked and closed the connection.

John went back to bed and slept a dreamless sleep.

Almost a year after her initial visit, John once again waited for Ms. Zhao. She would arrive in minutes, and was likely going through the "airlock" as they called it, right this moment.

John didn't know exactly why he cared so much, but he did. He wanted to show off what they had done, entirely within the contract Springbranch had committed to. And besides, she had been so businesslike except for that moment looking at the sky – he wanted to make that kind of connection again and see what an outsider really thought about their solution. She was coming at his request this time, not under the direction of her clients.

When her Auto pulled up, he stepped outside to meet her, handing her a bottle of Jose Cuervo. "For you," he said.

"Thanks?" she answered. She had on a light blouse and slacks this time. "I'm not a big tequila drinker."

"Well, this is good and you should try it," he said.

She was silent for a heartbeat, then said, "Okay. I will." She continued with a change of tone, "You do know that was a $5000 bottle I brought you before? Very rare."

Suddenly John was mortified. "Oh."

"It's not a problem. I didn't choose it. My clients did."

He let go of his tension. She was trying. "Go for a walk?"

"Of course," she replied.

They walked the same way they had before. It was after dusk and the stars were coming out.

"The stars, they're... different." She stopped in mid stride. "Wait, why do you have stars at all?"

"We had complete freedom about how to spend our city infrastructure money. There's more than one company that can steal a sky. The resolution and color is really pretty good, isn't it? You'd need a pretty decent telescope to tell the difference from the real thing."

"Hmmm..." she said. "My clients won't like this. They kind of like the idea that they control the lights of Springbranch."

"They have to abide by the contract, too, right? Besides, who will tell them?"

"They will find out sooner or later, but I'm not going to be the one to tell them," she said softly.

They walked again, enjoying the night.

"What sky is this?"

"The Atacama Desert, near Mt. Paranal, Chile, site of the old VLT—Very Large Telescope. I have it on genius authority that it's fantastic. Do you like it?"

She paused to look up. Several minutes passed.

"Yes," she said after a while. "What are those, to the south? The fuzzy looking things?"

John answered, "The Magellanic clouds, satellite galaxies to our own Milky Way."

"I like them very much," she said. "We don't get to see those in New York City."

"No," he agreed. "I don't suppose you do. But maybe we can share them.

Mike Brotherton is a professor of astronomy at the University of Wyoming where he investigates quasars, the most luminous active galactic nuclei. He uses the Hubble Space Telescope, the Very Large Array in New Mexico, and any other telescope that will grant him observing time. He is also the author of the science fiction novels Star Dragon and Spider Star, both from Tor Books, as well as a number of short stories and popular science articles. He is the founder of Launch Pad Astronomy Workshop for Writers, which brings professional writers to Wyoming every summer in order to better educate and inspire their audiences. He has edited the anthologies Diamonds in the Sky, Launch Pad (with Jody Lynn Nye) and Science Fiction by Scientists. His webpage is www.mikebrotherton.com.

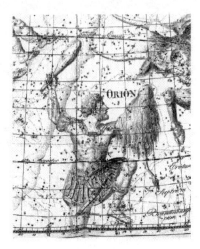

Seven Sisters

Jennifer Lee Rossman

When I was little, my favorite stories were the ones written in the stars. Fantastic tales of equally fantastic creatures and heroes that have been told since the beginning of time.

These were the first ever bedtime stories, my dad would say, on those precious nights when we would drive out to the desert with our telescope. And stories are what make us human. When we evolved enough curiosity to make shapes from the dots of light in the sky and the language to tell our families about them, that was the moment humanity started.

And it didn't just happen to one person in one place. No. All over the world, people started telling stories about the stars, like a switch flicked inside them all at once. That's how you get different tales about the same constellation: where Greece saw a woman in chains, Mesopotamia saw a demon, and the Marshall Islands saw a porpoise; what we call the Milky Way, the Khoisan people say are the embers a lonely little girl scattered in a dark sky. That's one of my favorites.

My favorite favorite, though, is the Pleiades.

Seven sisters who were chased by Orion for seven years, until their father turned them into doves and they flew up to the sky to become stars. Orion became stars, too, and he kept chasing them through the night sky. Zeus never let him get them, though, because he was all-powerful and would always protect them, like they were his own children.

On the night my father died, one of the seven stars goes out.

Light pollution, I tell myself. Or clouds. Even in perfect conditions, you can't always see all seven sisters.

But I had been able to see them all that night, even through my tears. They were all there, and then Merope just... disappeared.

She was always Orion's main infatuation, the reason he pursued her and her sisters. Had he finally caught her?

My heart goes out to the poor nymph whose father can't protect her anymore. She'd thought him immortal, but even gods die.

Okay, so maybe I'm projecting my feelings onto a ball of gas. Can you blame me? I'm a teenager, suddenly alone and lost in the world with nothing but the stars to guide her. And the stars, supposedly fixed and reliable, have just changed. That situation kind of lends itself to overdramatic personification of astronomical objects.

I step back from the telescope and take a deep breath. "There's a scientific explanation for everything," I tell myself, quoting Dad. For all his philosophical waxing about myths, the man is nothing if not a believer in science.

Was.

The word presses on my chest. I couldn't possibly forget that he's gone, but for a second, just a second, I'd almost convinced myself that he's right there in that old truck, eating snacks from that dorky fanny pack he always wore. That I hadn't driven out to the desert by myself from the hospital, in the driver's seat instead of the passenger's, music blaring so I wouldn't have to notice how quiet it was.

And now he's a was. Everything he is and says and loves, was and said and loved.

I wipe my eyes and look through the telescope again.

Sterope blinks out next. She was the dimmest of the sisters, but the sky still looks a little darker without her.

What is happening? Is there some sort of... craft? A balloon or something, blocking the light from the stars?

Celaeno and Electra join their sister, wherever they have gone.

I'd consider the possibility that something is happening to the actual stars, but they wouldn't just go out. They would get brighter before going supernova. And besides, they aren't actually close to each other; it only looks that way from my position on Earth. In reality, they're light-years away from each other. Even if something happened to them all at once, the light from the event would reach us at vastly different times. Years, decades would pass between the times we would see Alcyone and Maia go out.

And yet Alcyone and Maia disappear within seconds of each other, then finally Taygeta.

A few stars in the cluster remain, but the seven sisters are gone.

I knew I wouldn't have him forever. No matter what the stories say, no one is immortal, and no matter what gods you pray to, none of them are going to come down and cure the brain tumor of some random astrophysics professor. Not even the ones with daughters who really need them.

I should have known, I think, as I lay in the bed of the truck, my head resting on a pile of Dad's clothes, eating snacks from his fanny pack as I stare at that black space. I should have known that the gods would have no mercy for him, because they don't care. How could they? Look at Zeus, pretending to protect the Pleiades from Orion, only to give him a place of honor in the stars, forever chasing those scared little girls.

Dad wasn't just my father and best friend. He was my guardian, too, keeping away all the bad things that chased me. But sometimes, the bad things get you anyway.

Little lights flicker in the distance, hovering like fireflies on the horizon, where the stark black silhouettes of the mountains carve jagged shapes into the night sky.

Seven little flickering lights.

I sit up, watching as they swoop down toward Earth, twirling and twining around one another as they zip across the desert, illuminating the gentle curves of sand and dirt.

"Impossible," I mutter. Stars are enormous, burning balls of gas. They can't fall to Earth.

Yet here they come, growing larger and brighter as they approach, skimming the ground side-by-side. I stand up in the bed of the truck, squinting, and try to gauge their size. Car headlights? Flashlights? By the time they're close enough for me to tell they're each the size of the truck and show no signs of slowing down, there's no time to run.

I hunker down, arms over my head and eyes squeezed shut as their white glow brightens even though my eyelids. An image from a history book pops into my head: permanent shadows left in the wake of a nuclear blast.

Just when I think the lights can't get any brighter, they abruptly go out. There's a soft rustle of feathers, like birds flying past my head.

Dark spots dance in front of my eyes when I dare open them, but I see the ghostly images of white birds flitting through the moonlight.

The Pleiades were turned to doves before they became stars. But there's no way....

More flickering lights appear on the horizon. These lack the playful grace of the Pleiades, arranging themselves into the form of a man, sword in hand and trademarked belt slung across his hips as he clumbers toward me.

A glance at the sky reveals another starless patch where Orion should be.

He's coming for them.

The doves circle me, drawing closer with each pass until I can feel the wind on my face. They land of the truck, some perched on the cab, others nestled in Dad's clothes. They all stare at me, their little bodies heaving with every panting breath.

"You finally got away," I say quietly. "But I don't know what you expect from me. I can't protect you."

They coo sadly in unison.

"My dad would know what to do," I tell them. "He always knew how to deal with bullies."

I hate how easy it is to use past tense already. Like he's been gone forever instead of just a few hours.

But the Pleiades need someone to protect them, and I guess that someone is me. Dad is gone, but his wisdom lives on inside of me. I can do this, I can figure out what he would do if he were here.

How I wish he were here, not just to help but because he would have loved this so much. He would list all the reasons it's impossible, thoroughly and scientifically debunk the entire thing... and then he'd grin, his eyes sparkling, and tell me it doesn't matter if it's possible or not. None of the stories we tell about the stars are possible, but if it's a good story, it can change everything.

That's what he would do. Tell a story. And if he didn't know any stories about that particular star I'd point out, he'd make one up, just like the first humans did.

Orion is maybe a hundred yards away now, his stars glowing in a vaguely human shape that towers toward the sky. The Pleiades turn away from him, listening raptly as I make up a story.

Once there was a girl who loved the stars almost as much as she loved her father. She lost both on the same night, because maybe her father really was a god, and maybe it was him that kept the stars in the sky.

For millennia, Orion had chased the Pleiades through the heavens, but when the girl's father died and the seven sisters fell to Earth, Zeus wasn't around to protect them anymore. Orion saw his chance. He leapt to Earth and chased them.

But the girl had an idea. They needed a new hero in the stars.

So the Pleiades took her father's belongings and they fled back to the empty patch of sky, forever immortalizing him in the stars.

When Orion chased them, he saw that someone more worthy had taken his place. With nowhere for him to fit in, Orion broke apart, streaming through the sky as a meteor shower.

The girl looked up, watching as the seven Pleiades reclaimed their spot in the heavens. The sky looked much the same as it had the night before, but she could see the difference.

Ancient Babylonia called him a shepherd. The Lakota saw him as a bison. Most of the world still called him Orion. They saw him as a mighty hunter carrying a sword and wearing a belt. But the girl knew better.

That was no sword, but a telescope. And the belt? That was really a dorky fanny pack full of snacks to sustain the hero as he watched over Earth, the heavens, and his little girl.

Jennifer Lee Rossman is an autistic, disabled, and queer writer from Binghamton, New York. She's not entirely sure if her story is a metaphor, either. She tweets @JenLRossman

Moon Cakes

Salinda Tyson

She hid in the hollow hornbeam tree because the smell of stag's blood on the late winter air had drawn a wolf. She cursed, unwilling to fight the beast for a greater share of meat. Her cold hands had made butchering slow. When the wolf had fed and padded away into the forest, she frantically harvested what she could drag back to her cottage by moonlight and starlight. She lit a lantern and yelled to scare off the foxes and lynx that watched from the dark woods.

The brilliant pinprick stars of the Hunter and his hound stood above the rooftree of her home when she returned, almost as if striding over her roof. She frowned at the pattern of glittering white sparks in the blackness overhead, knowing and fearing their possible meanings. Hunter or hunted? She had not read the stars in a long time. Doubt gnawed at her. Was she still safe here? She half expected to hear the thump of boots on the thatch as if the Sky Hunter himself had come visiting.

But it was a mortal man who came the next evening, swinging down from his iron-shod war horse. A big, confident man, with curly black hair, who walked toward her, forcing her against the wall of her cottage. A guardsman from the fortress on the crag, long sword strapped on his left side, short sword on his right side, his leather jerkin salt-stained and pungent with both human and horse sweat.

What could she say? Or do? She was a peasant, a barterer of herbal remedies and love potions, who sometimes tended the sick, or acted as midwife.

"What have you for me, witch?" he asked. His lip curled, his eyes darkened.

"That depends on what you want," she said, meeting his eyes.

He took her arm, pulled her to him. "Inside woman, and get to work, unless you want it against a tree."

He sniffed out the honeyberry tart she had cooling by the window, and devoured half of it before stating his business.

He reminded her of a stag, the ones she had seen in the forest barking and challenging other stags for their harem of does, lowering their antlered heads and charging, clashing together with a sound like thunder. Once she had discovered, deep in a part of the woods where only she ventured, a pair of wounded males locked together, tongues lolling, fallen onto their sides, the branches and tines of their great antlers locked together, condemning them to die, each bound to the other. Twilight was coming and a wolf sat patiently under a hornbeam tree across the meadow, observing and waiting. He looked to be an old, seasoned wolf, poised with his tail across his paws, wise enough to be wary of those dagger-sharp points of the bucks' antlers, and patient enough to wait for his supper of stag's blood licked from a ravaged throat and venison ripped from the already scored flanks of the combatants.

Bala watched the stags. She watched the wolf. She nodded to both, acknowledging the cycles of life and death, the majesty and indifference of nature. And considering how much meat she could harvest from the two great, heaving bodies, even after the wolf had taken its portion. And what ladles and tools, knife handles and buttons and implements she could fashion from those two glorious pairs of antlers. It was only a matter of time.

She had waited and watched, let the wolf eat its fill, and scavenged when it was safe.

Tarik's intended was not paying him the attention he desired, so he demanded yet another love potion. "Make her fancy me," he whispered. This he told her after he had smacked his lips over the pie, pulled her hair and slapped her. She wondered: Was this how he would treat his intended, a high-born lady whose father could dower her with an estate and lands rich in game, fields and orchards and serfs aplenty? She pressed her lips tight together, repressing her anger and repulsion, and pondering. Bending the will was a dark magic, a step along the darker path. In truth, she half pitied the lady he desired, though she considered herself moon-struck to pity any gentlefolk. She had only glimpsed the lady in question peeking from an ornate litter and sitting on a palfrey, a slight figure, with a soft voice and long, thin hands, hiking up the skirts of an overdress.

His narrowed eyes were a warning.

"A potion that works," he growled. "Or damn you, witch, I'll drive you out, make you wish you had never been born."

"My price is—"

"Your price? Ha, you give me what I want and I swear I do you no harm. You know very well you should be grateful for that." He sneered in contempt. He strode across the room, closed his sword hand about her neck and squeezed. She choked, gasped for air. He raised his arm a bit. Her feet no longer touched the floor. She focused on the dark blur of hair on his hand, and the crumb of pie crust in the edge of his beard. After a few seconds, he relaxed his grip, grinning at her.

He likes to see fear, she thought. *The doom in the eyes of prey.* Her feet scrabbled for purchase on the floor. Struggling to speak, she cleared her throat. Stars swam before her eyes.

"You swear, Sir Tarik," she croaked, "if I give you what you want, you will do me no further harm?" She stared into his eyes. "Swear by the moon and sun."

His lips curled. A gob of dark honeyberry was smeared beside his mouth. "I swear by the moon and sun, witch."

He stalked away to his horse, wiping his hands on his jerkin, as if touching her had polluted him.

As he rode away, she sighed in relief, and leaned over her worktable, shaking. She dipped a cloth in a pail of cool water and held it against her neck. She closed her eyes and ground her teeth. She had lusted after the honeyberry pie all day, mixing the berries and dried apples and mint, rolling out the dough, daydreaming of the taste, and now she would have to force herself to eat it.

Why did men even want magics to ensure that the women they fancied loved them in return? Vanity? A lack of confidence? A belief that there was something of sorcery in the bond of regard and love itself? She shook her head. That even a man like Tarik would seek a love-charm! Did it show a softer side of him? Did he wish simply to control the lady, to bind her to him, or did he truly desire her affection?

Thomas the archer's shoulders were massively muscled from a lifetime of pulling the great yew bow, a weapon that made the lord's army so feared. Sometimes he hunted and brought her meat, never the rich venison that always went to the lord's table, but rabbits and squirrels and wild ducks. And he required a certain kind of payment in return.

He turned to her as they lay together on her pallet, talking afterward, telling her a tale to which she at first paid little attention. He had joined Tarik's company of soldiers on border raids and shared in the loot, so he expected his standing in life to improve. He too had a lady love in mind. Not her. A smith's daughter. He went on and on about this other. As if she had no feelings, as if it did not matter to her that he was imagining another, dreaming of another, even while he lay in bed beside her.

She sniffed and turned away from him.

He touched her shoulder.

"Angry, are you? Well, you should not be. You know the world is hard and poor folk must shift for themselves." He rolled onto his back, shaking his head, and laughed. "Now then. You know this is only truth." He touched her shoulder as if in regret. "I'm sorry, Bala girl."

She wanted to strike him, pull his brindle hair from his head, but coiled her anger deep inside, like banking embers of a fire so it lasts through the night for baking in the morning.

Thomas shrugged. "After all, you're... what you are. And I do pay you."

A day later, he stepped from the woods and asked for a charm to be sure of the smith's daughter. He gave her a fat wild goose, as if that would pay for all her troubles. As if that would excuse the wound in her heart.

His actions hurt her more than Tarik's. Because he understood her. His folk were like hers—poor foot soldiers, foresters, wise women, those who did others' bidding and bowed their heads; he knew well that marrying a reputed witch was unwise. Did he care for her or was he simply using her skills to climb higher in the social order? She felt her heart shrivel.

She stared into his eyes. "Swear you will not cry me out as a witch if I give you a charm. Swear by the moon and sun."

He nodded. "I swear by the moon and sun, Bala."

While he dozed, she went outside to peer at the stars.

Now to fix moon cakes—for both men. First, she went into the forest, as if pulled there, to the oldest, most sacred oak groves. A dark anger grew in her, rising like a coiled snake. She filled her basket with a dozen different kinds of acorns that blanketed the floor of the woods, a small sample of the richness of this place that she could carry with her. She gathered twigs, berries, bark, mosses, and medicinal plants, all helpful on a journey. At dusk she dragged the loaded basket and bundles of plants and switches back on a crude sledge she had fashioned. She would not ask Thomas to bring her a pony to ease the task or rouse his questions.

The recipe was her mother's and grandmother's, taught to her when she was a child. Two large cakes would require all the meal she had prepared earlier. To make her own supply, first she broke and split the acorn shells to harvest the nutmeats. She set aside the shells to use later for dyeing, and roasted the yellow-orange meats. Kneeling at the mortar stone, she ground the split nutmeats. The half-prepared meal was a yellow rich as egg yolks. Grinding and grinding, she worked the pestle stone back and forth in circles and spirals until the meal sifted through her fingers like golden flour. She rinsed and leached it in many changes of water to destroy the bitter taste. Her muscles remembered every step of the work. She dipped a fingertip in and licked off a few delicious morsels of the sweet meal before pouring it into a small traveling sack.

She stretched and sighed.

The earlier prepared flour she divided in two parts, blended a goose egg into each lot of meal, worked in sweet butter, and stirred in cool spring water. Next she poured in honey from her own hives, and sprinkled in pinches of precious cinnamon and ginger and pepper she had received from a maid in the lord's kitchen, as payment for a stay-home spell put on an errant husband.

She took a curled hair from Tarik's sword hand that had caught on her clothes when he choked her. Another from his head, a long, dark hair thick as thread. Chanting, she drew her sharpest knife and cut the hairs into segments small as fish roe, or specks of pepper, then blended them carefully into the cake she intended for him. To Thomas's cake, she added only one hair from his head that she cut fine and blended into the dough.

She raked the embers of her hearth fire, wrapped the round loaves in wet leaves, and slid them into a shallow pot in the ashes. The sweet, rich smell made her mouth water. So like the aroma of kitchens where her mother and her grandmother had baked pies and special cakes. But she knew she could not nibble a crumb from either of these cakes.

The snort of Tarik's stallion gave him away. She nodded a greeting as he entered the clearing.

Swiftly, she ducked inside her door, and twisted to face him, pointing to the hearth deep with ashes, where the seductive smell of baking lingered.

"Moon cake," she said. She scooped up the one she had made for him, opening the wrapping and offering him the round, warm, fragrant shape the color of the sun in fog.

"So I simply eat it?" he asked, eyeing her. He sniffed in appreciation.

"Yes, tonight *after* sup. You've brought a napkin you used to wipe your mouth and hands at supper to wrap it in?" He nodded. "Keep it wrapped. Best to look at the moon as you eat it all down. Every crumb."

Her instructions to Thomas were the same. He thanked her but looked somewhat shamefaced. "Ah, Bala, you're a witch. No man will marry you. You know that." He touched her shoulder. "The world is what it is. But I am sorry for that." Then he was gone, his bow over his shoulder.

At dusk, after she had prepared her pack, her walking stick, her bow and arrows, herbs, teas, snares, and flints, she walked into the forest to the grove. At midnight, when the full moon was overhead, she drew a circle centered on the hornbeam tree. She whispered into the shadows beneath the trees and to the bright face of the moon:

"Open mouths, Take this food within
become other selves in other skins."

Next day near twilight, from inside her shelter in the hollow tree, Bala heard the horn and the belling of hounds. Hunters pounded through the meadows and fields, into the forest.

A huge stag with an odd black hide had been spotted and the lord's huntsman had loosed the dogs. One, a brindle coat never seen before in the kennels, led the pack. It ran swift as an arrow—and, snarling, forced the great stag to whirl at bay.

But abruptly the big, brindle-coated hound bent its muzzle to the ground, sniffing, as if seeking another trail. It whined deep in its throat, pacing back and forth, and circling, as if in pain or scenting something strange. The huntsmen cursed, lashing it on, and it leapt onto the stag's back, clawing and bloodying it. The pack bayed and swarmed over the black stag's flanks, slavering, tearing, feasting.

Twisting its head, the stag stared at her with its great brown eyes as if puzzled. A look of human horror and betrayal veiled the animal eyes for an instant.

She closed her eyes for a second and swallowed. Her heart pounded.

Tarik likes to see fear, she thought. So I see his fear and the doom in his eyes as he becomes prey.

Struggling, the beast snorted and barked, stumbling to its knees but unable to rise, lowering its great head to slash the onrushing hounds. Its antlers ripped deep into the brindle hound's flank, which yelped in pain with an almost human sound, but rejoined the pack's mad rush. The hound whined as it was flung against a tree. Bone snapped.

Safe inside the tree, Bala's throat burned with bile. The magic had taken its own way, chosen a more twisted path than she had intended.

Despite its broken back, the dying hound crawled toward the tree that concealed her, pleading in its eyes, an understanding of what she had done. The stag's eyes also met hers. It tried one final time to stumble upright. But the magic kept the spell-beasts from reaching her as they lay dying. All three were bound by the iron circle of sorcery. Before she had only used small magics, not spells that extended her will and hatred, and summoned and harnessed elemental forces....

She shuddered. Too late to turn aside from the midnight path. Had the stars led her into darkness? The Sky Hunter appeared as a waking dream before her—his hound, his bow, his stern face, his eyes twin blazing points of light.

She wept a tear for Thomas, licked the salt from her lips. If only she had a moon cake to fill her belly, but she would have to travel hungry. Eyes wide, she watched from her secret shelter inside the cloven hornbeam tree. The full moon would light her way home, for she knew the woods well. And the full moon, and what she had gathered from the forest, would aid her flight. Because when all spirit left their bodies and the stag and brindle hound truly died, when the moon was directly overhead, the spell would also die, and their awful remains would transform. Thomas would be found in the woods, perhaps by the smith or his daughter, his body bloody, his back broken. And for those at the lord's high table tonight? Diners thrusting knives into succulent venison haunch might think they were carving a human side, a man's thigh.

Bitterly, she smiled. She had her revenge on two scornful men. But she would be hunted as mercilessly as the stag had been, killed as brutally as the hound.

If she were caught.

Salinda Tyson has dipped her toes in the Susquehanna River, ducked under a library table during the Loma Prieta earthquake, marveled at ancient Roman aqueducts in France, strolled along Hadrian's Wall in the North of England, enjoyed double rainbows in Germany, and walked 500 paces around banyan trees in Florida. She is a long-term fan of fantasy and mythology. Her work appears in several Third Flatiron anthologies, Abyss & Apex, and Shadows in Salem.

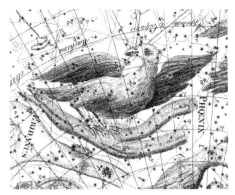

Blow the Stars Away

Andrew Leon Hudson

Two and a half years after Nightfall, more or less, the person responsible abandoned his life and left for Argentina.

Fled, some would say. The newscasts certainly did, speculating urgently about where the infamous Farmer Soth had gone.

Aimée would have quickly pointed out that one flees *from* something, not *towards.* Ji-Hu would have responded that one flees to safety. Aimée would say that was justification in itself; it was bad enough that governmental committees the world over had laid all blame at his feet, let alone how the entire scientific community had scapegoated him personally and joined the lynch-mob in baying for blood; who wouldn't want to seek refuge from that? Ji-Hu (the only person to whom he had actually confided his destination, in part specifically to facilitate their arguments in his absence) would thank her for conceding the debate.

Farmer wasn't there to enjoy the escalating banter that would follow between them, the furious digressions that would bud off from it, and later all the rolling around, of course; he was busy already having left, or fled, if one preferred. But he knew it would happen.

You could change the world for the blink of an eye, change the universe for*ever,* but it wouldn't change people, not deep down.

He departed by stages, by nations. After a week in the freshly minted Republic of Catalunya, Barcelona always being easy to lose oneself in, he bought individual flights to São Paulo, Brazil; then Santiago, Chile; and finally into Argentina, changing at Buenos Aires for the final leg to Neuquén, the largest city in Patagonia. Forty-eight hour jet-lag was an acceptable price to pay to increase a slim chance of future anonymity.

Despite his travel-worn state, plus the fourteen years since their last encounter, Mateo Tiago Roja recognized him from a distance, bounding to his feet with a cheer, wrapping him in a bear hug, holding him back for scrutiny, hugging him again.

"Good to see you, Farmer," he muttered, in an unexpected moment of half-discretion, then releasing him continued at full volume, endlessly voluble as he draped a heavy arm across Farmer's shoulders, guiding him towards the airport exit. "*John*, this is not your only luggage, you're staying longer than this, I hope? Come, I have a car for us, you must tell me everything, how are those lovely ladies of yours—*ha!*—I shouldn't say *ladies*, I know, but how could you not bring them...."

The car was, in fact, a lavishly stretched Hum-Vee, all cream leather and tinted glass. Like stepping up into a millionaire's mobile den, Farmer thought, which of course was exactly what it was. "It looks like you've done as well as you always said you would."

"Inevitable, my friend, inevitable." Time had added comfortable kilos to Mateo from head to toe, but his blue eyes, thick surfer-blond fringe and toothy grin remained unchanged. "You look fabulous," he said, smoothing tailored trousers across thick thighs.

Farmer smiled in spite of himself. Even back in their student days, Mateo had a way of preening when he paid someone else a compliment, constantly aware (or at least convinced) that he was the best-looking man at any gathering. "And you're a terrible mess, as always."

Mateo's laugh boomed. "Come, *John*, let's drink a toast to the late, lamented Professor Farmer Soth, eh? I feel so good to see you, it's almost like you didn't end the world at all!"

Everyone in the collider control center looked at each other, then started checking the systems logs, the sensor readouts, anything that would explain the momentary blackout that had dropped the room into darkness. Barely a flicker, if it had happened at all—Farmer really couldn't tell.

"Did we have a power-cut?" he asked, but he could tell just by the fact that the computer screens reported all systems still working that it wasn't the case. *It wasn't a blink,* he told himself.

He was tempted to put everything on hold, but it seemed there was nothing to demand any delay. The firing had occurred; the immediate simplified output from the observation array came in, *and matched the predictions;* the vast mass of full data had been acquired and stored— no way to know if there had been some interruption to the collection process, compromising their rewards, but no evidence to suggest there had been. No one reported any reason not to go ahead with the second firing. So, exactly twenty minutes after the first time, he gave the order, and they did.

The room fell into blackness a second time, surely for less than the blink of an eye. They all noticed, all looked at each other warily. "Let's hold off on another for now," he said.

He couldn't have known that half the world's population had begun screaming again.

Farmer spent a month doing nothing but catching the sun and growing his beard. When away from his work, Mateo engaged in copious recreation until the only indulgence gone untapped was sleep. The grounds around his sprawling house contained gardens that were genuinely beautiful, as well as a tennis court and a large swimming pool; the house itself had a cinema and wine cellar in the basement, all of it at his old friend's disposal.

Farmer had a corner of the house to himself, a huge bedroom boasting an en suite bathroom larger than the one he'd once shared with Aimée and Ji-Hu, a private lounge with a patio balcony that featured a small jacuzzi and a breakfast-and-wet-bar kept well-stocked by unseen staff. If he wished, he could go a week without seeing anyone; some days his encounters with Mateo were no more than a called greeting over the balcony rail. The invitations to join in his thriving social life always went politely refused.

By the end of that month he was going stir crazy, but exploring brought him no ease. Neuquén—or at least the part of it Mateo lived in—recalled the worst aspects of the wealthy northern hemisphere. The affluent suburbs were a jigsaw of gated neighborhoods, a palimpsest of walled-in mansions, the expansive gardens within seemingly the domain of attack dogs instead of people, private security vehicles cruising the pristine empty streets. A casual walk was all but impossible; Mateo had stared at him like he was mad just for suggesting it.

"It's the gas money," he confided one evening, after he returned from a long hard day of earning more of it. "We sit here upon one of the richest shale gas and oil reserves in the world. Well, the reserves are out at Vaca Muerta. It's the money that sits here—" he spread a wide smile "—and we upon it."

Farmer shook his head. "I always thought you'd get rich flogging a dead horse."

Mateo roared, then recovered himself to sudden seriousness. "There have been burglaries, kidnappings even. Not in this zone of course, our security is the finest, I wouldn't have let you go wandering otherwise, but still. There are some who are jealous of those of us who made the wise decisions and benefit from them as we do."

"And you don't think it would be better to share that wealth around?"

"Ha-hah! After all these years, another campus debate for us, yes? Let me unmask your eyes to the corruption and incompetence that our so-called *government* would shame themselves with, if only they had their hand in the jar! No, no, they might claim to work for the greater good, but the money would still fill someone else's private pocket, less deserving even than I." Mateo swallowed wine, and gave him a knowing look. "Besides, we see what happens when idealists get too much money thrown at them...."

It was meant as a jibe between friends, but it hit hard, and Mateo realized instantly. "Forgive me, Farmer, I apologies. And, look, I swear to you, it's not just houses and cars the money goes to. You need a break from here? Go visit Alto Valle, see what I have them doing there. You will like it, I think, a lot more than outside around here. You have to promise me, no more of that, okay? Not in the daytime, and definitely not at night."

But Farmer didn't need warning not to leave the grounds after dark, and safety had nothing to do with it. He avoided the gardens even, and always drew the curtains to his suite before sunset.

He didn't believe the call when it came—how could anyone?—and by the time he and his unwitting team had been lured outside, or to anywhere with a window even, there was nothing to suggest that this day had been unlike any other. The high clouds raced a little more than they had that morning, perhaps, and the research campus was unusually quiet, the car park empty for so early in the afternoon.

But when the control room landline rang and he heard the nonsense it spouted, and as his team turned on cellphones and laughed at what *had* to be hoaxes hailing from every corner of the globe, and when they found that mainstream newsfeeds were carrying the same impossible pictures and videos that social media was....

Some departed straight away to be with their loved ones; others drifted off as the hours passed, but a few were still with him as dusk drew in, the sun set, and the blue Swiss sky deepened into night.

The day had seemed the same as all the rest, but it was a night like none other in history.

A crescent moon rose into a sky that was perfectly clear, and utterly starless.

Farmer accepted Mateo's offer of a car from Neuquén to Alto Valle, but only long enough to drop him off. Mateo tried to force it on him as a gift, stupid wealth making him oblivious to the fact that Farmer wasn't impoverished by any means—he simply wanted to become one more ordinary person in the once-ordinary world, instead of notorious, or despised.

In any case, the granting of other rich man's favors were gifts enough.

The director of AgriBosque S.A. looked like he'd never set foot indoors in his life: a lean, hearty man in his fifties, face deeply tanned, lined like sandstone worked by centuries of erosion. Yet here they were, in the foyer of a small, bright, single-story building that served as corporate headquarters for what Mateo called "my little guilt project."

"I'm Alejandro Minguez," the man said, shaking hands. "Welcome."

"John Farmer." He half choked on the name, but it wasn't the new identity which had been created for him that gave him pause. Minguez's grip was leathery and firm, and it had been a long time since any stranger had offered Farmer their hand.

"Señor Roja said to expect a new employee, but not what you'd be doing for us."

Farmer hesitated awkwardly. "To tell you the truth, I'm a little hazy on that myself."

Minguez took it in his stride. "What kind of things do you usually do?"

"Well, I suppose you could say monitoring systems, computers... I've done some electrical engineering. But honestly, I'll be happy to do anything you ask me to."

The older man smiled, and gestured to the door. "Well, let me give you the tour. Maybe we'll come up with something."

AgriBosque was based on the periphery of Alto Valle, the office surrounded by attractive gardens designed to charm visitors. The community itself was only like Neuquén in that, from above, it would appear a patchwork; but where the rich suburbs had been cross-hatched by walls of reinforced brick, here the land was blanketed with farms, and the highest walls were formed by lines of trees.

The longest of them stretching beyond sight.

Farmer would see their far end for himself, in time. But to begin with there was only the office and the gardens, and a small town surrounded by green, mostly populated by people who worked hard through the day and slept sound right through the night.

That sounded pretty good.

In the moment of the first firing, the light went out.

Not the illumination in the tunnels of the collider ring, nor the campus complex where the control room was housed; nor the towns and villages that occupied the countryside above it for miles around, nor the cities, here and around the world. Not merely the world itself, gold-gleaming scatter across its darkened hemisphere.

The *light*.

A passing yet fundamental effect, a subtle wave in the quanta of space-time, expanded from that collision point. Before it, the visible spectrum collapsed—or were the flying particles consumed, fueling the wave's growth?

In the tunnels, in the control center, everywhere, blackness reigned. But for only a moment, and then every LED and bulb shone again, light flooded rooms, streets, roads. On the far side of the planet, in the depth of night, at first it seemed like no more than a blip of the grid—until they saw the great absence overhead, not even the moon hanging lonely in the black.

But those basking on the dayside watched the sun extinguished.

They witnessed, uncomprehending, as the wave erased all light falling on the earth. They looked out from the center of an ever-expanding sphere through which no photons passed, within which an instant, absolute night had fallen. For a terrible moment it was as to be struck blind, only to be rescued by the precious glimmer of automated streetlights warming to life, or the screen of a television or fumbled cell phone lighting up shocked and staring faces.

It took eight minutes and twenty seconds for the wave to pass the sun. Only then, once it, too, was within the sphere of the wave, could sunlight resume its achingly slow journey back.

Finally, in an instant, day burst back into existence, the empty black of the sky filled out with blue, and the six billion people then directly under the sun emerged from rioting chaos into clamorous relief. Whatever collective nightmare had taken place, it was over.

Except, just under three and a half minutes later, Farmer gave the order to re-fire and it all happened again.

Farmer got up a little after dawn, habitual now, despite having been for so many years a night owl. He pulled on Crocs forever caked with dust or mud, and a set of hard-wearing denim overalls worn to comfort over the last few years. Breakfast was black coffee and a potato flatcake, plus—for the next few weeks at least—whatever they felt like plucking from a low-hanging limb on their way to the forest wall.

In spite of near constant winds blowing down off the Andes—hard, dry winds that would beat any fruit tree into barren submission—bountiful pear and apple orchards flourished back in Alto Valle, sheltered in the lee of layered rows of tall poplars. They were irrigated via shallow channels periodically flooded from canals fed by the Río Negro and Río Limay to the west, and spaced widely enough that cattle could be grazed in between. Herds were rotated through different areas to allow the grassed undergrowth to lie fallow and regrow, and the poplars could be cut and replanted over time.

Staggered harvests of fruit, livestock, and wood—agroforestry was a long-established farming strategy, delivering a variety of sustainable incomes. Mateo's capacity to invest had simply taken it to another level. AgriBosque S.A. had expanded the concept that had allowed Alto Valle to endure and extended it far over the southern horizon, long bands of man-made forest protecting narrow strips of orchard each tens of kilometers in length.

Farmer worked in a team of eight, one of many herding the animals that grazed between the trees and on the patch of open plains that surrounded them, slowly working their way up and down the forest wall until they were ready for slaughter. A couple of gauchos brought the cattle in from the plain each morning, and rode their handsome criollos back and forth along the treeline to keep them from drifting off again, while the other six hands cycled through tasks: three kept an eye on the herd within the forest; two more worked in the orchards of their current zone; and the last cooked, cleaned and kept in contact with the company from whichever bunkhouse they were currently based out of.

Farmer was also responsible for setting up mobile shock fencing at the north and south extremes of their temporary range, ensuring the herd didn't disappear into the trees before they were ready to move them on. Old Minguez had just about kept a straight face when he mentioned that electrical engineering was going to come in handy after all.

Farmer was content to work his tasks and work on his Spanish, to the extent that eventually his crewmates only laughed when he was actually sharing a story or joke. He rarely spoke to anyone outside the company—even Mateo, feeling awkward on those few occasions when the man bankrolling his new life called to check he hadn't tired of it and wanted to come actually enjoy himself for a change.

He didn't read, listen to, or watch the news or much of anything else. He had no interest in the world, was quite happy for it to go on without him, trying not to count the days down.

And then he had a visitor.

"You sought to play God, sir, to wield god-like powers, but with only man's fallibility to guide you. And you've brought punishment down, a devilish punishment. Not just on yourself, but on us all."

There was no righteous applause at this—the righteous were all long-since clapped out—but that made it worse somehow: the long, full chamber just barely echoing with this last voice of condemnation, the figures to either side of the speaker not even nodding their assent.

He'd taken the blows. If he didn't hide his face, he was castigated for a lack of shame. If he looked away, he was excoriated for failing to meet his accusers' gaze. If he spoke, he was shouted down. If he was silent, that silence spoke deafeningly of unquestionable guilt.

When Lennon sang "above us only sky" it was meant as a thing of wonder, of celebration. Now that sky was all there was above, the material heavens had become a solely oppressive thing instead, featureless except for the sun and a precious handful of lonely planets and moons, the fleeting scar of a comet or meteor.

It didn't matter that it wasn't his intent, it was what had happened.

He didn't blame the people and their representatives for their outrage, no more than he blamed his peers for abandoning him. He had stolen the beauty of the night sky from the human eye; from the scientists, he had all but stolen science itself. Whole fields of research had become unworkable in an instant—telescopes stared into a true void now—but the damage went deeper. Distrust of science spread everywhere: another reactionary wave that carried protests and violence on its surge and left disenfranchisement of the learned, sometimes even deaths in its wake.

He was given up by his fellows as a sacrificial offering, in the hope that the eternal goal of future progress could yet be salvaged by the rest, and he couldn't fault them for doing so. Just the sight of him was a reminder of everything that had been lost. They *ought* to hate him. And, as his twin waves of darkness spread out across the universe, why too wouldn't he be cursed by beings as yet unguessed at, whom humanity might never meet?

Wouldn't it be better for all if he were to vanish as well?

"You know, after you'd been gone for a year, I got pretty pissed off with you."

Aimée showed up riding a rented electric trike powered via solar-sensitive paint, with an eco-engine for bad weather backup that ran on recycled cooking oil. She had a self-inflating/self-packing tent and a trailer loaded with supplies, so he cried off from the team and they headed up the forest wall for an hour or so before making camp.

She turned his face this way and that, prodding at the sun-creases around his eyes, tugging at his hair and beard like she expected them to come away and reveal the way he'd used to be. She looked just like she had before, despite the various ways she didn't.

"How's Ji-Hu?" he asked after they ate. She hadn't brought up their absent partner.

"They're fine. But we annulled the contract, so congratulations, you're now officially single. It was amicable, and we got on fine without you, by the way. So don't go imagining that the split is on you, the way you do with everything else. Anyway, we still talk, and last month I finally got them to say where you headed off to. As soon as they said 'Argentina' I knew the fat peacock would be part of it."

Farmer laughed. She'd been calling Mateo that even before he got, as he preferred to put it, *heavy-set*. He knew Mateo would have blanked anyone else with ease, but even snow would turn pale in the face of Aimée's controlled fury.

"Are you still pissed off?"

"Not for years, you idiot. We both knew why you went, and we couldn't have come with, and it would have been worse to try and talk about it all before, so."

"Are you happy?"

"I should be asking you." She scrutinized him in the glow from the portable stove, and abruptly he realized that dusk was falling. He felt a stab of agoraphobia at the anti-weight of the empty sky overhead.

But he looked up.

The sun had dropped below the shoulders of the mountain range. With the moon not risen to compete with it, sunset was like drawing back a curtain's edge of green-amber light from the pure darkening purple. No planets were visible. Almost exactly due north, a single point of light slowly but detectably shifted above the horizon, the ISS most likely. Far to the west, a contrail shone like a thread of gold, still catching the sun from behind the Andes.

And that was all.

Aimée grunted, as if something had been said that meant the matter was settled. "Any of those cowboys back there crawl into your bedroll of a night?" she asked.

He laughed again, she had always been good at making that happen. "No."

"Good. Because we're long overdue break-up sex, and I don't sleep with cheaters."

Later, when night was actually fallen, he woke and found himself seeing for the first time what was called the last man-made wonder of the world: the pin-prick glittering of orbital junk tumbling above the atmosphere, reflecting down the light in the wake of sundown and that brief spell before dawn. A sprinkling of miniscule flecks that had been invisible before the night sky was wiped clear, even now only seen from the corner of your eye against the featureless black where the Milky Way used to turn, gone the moment you looked right at them.

Ghosts of what he had taken away.

Six years after he left for Argentina, almost eight-and-a-half after Nightfall, and four months after Aimée rode off on her trike again, Farmer took his long-unclaimed holiday entitlement and headed south. He rode the coach to Bariloche, nearly six hours through grasslands and scrublands beneath the loom of the Andes, alongside the Río Negro as it snaked, and swelled into lakes, and then snaked again.

The running wasn't smooth, the wealth bestowed on Argentina by shale gas was still only helping Mateo and his kith. The crumbling blacktop was flanked on both sides by a strangely sparkling haze, and when the coach paused at a convenience stop to allow those onboard to stretch their legs and feed, he investigated and found a narrow, endless graveyard of discarded plastic bottles and aluminum cans, tossed from passing vehicles down the years. He kicked through them and the dust beneath, immediately uncovering ancient shells from the seabed Patagonia once had been, now covered over by mankind's unchanging contribution to the future.

It was the off-season, and Bariloche was relatively quiet, the skiing crowd not due for half a year. No problem to rent a hillside cabin, no problem at all—difficult to insist on a modest option, even, with more luxurious opportunities readily available. But all he wanted was seclusion, and the simpler the better: a place with no people, no connectivity.

Nothing to distract from what he'd come to see.

He went walking through steep forest, getting to know the best clearings, but as the day approached the weather began to work against him. Unusual humidity fueled cloud formation, and for the final three days it blanketed the sky, roiling past under the constant wind, any breaks in the cover too fleeting or wrongly timed.

The most important night of his life came, and went, and left him still unknowing.

He could have gone back, the rest of the world would know by now, but he couldn't bring himself to return. He had to find out for himself, this time to see the change he'd wrought with his own eyes.

After ten days more—the food he'd brought up from Bariloche all but gone—he woke to a pure blue dawn. The day passed out of his memory as fast as it entered. Later, he wouldn't recall leaving the cabin, only that he was waiting in a clearing when the sun went down, the glittering trail of space junk fading in its wake.

Night fell.

No racing planes while he watched, that night, no space stations or satellites. No moon, no planets. No clouds.

Only the black.

That, and the thing he had been waiting for, the certainty—so he hoped—that had drawn him to the southern hemisphere. Somewhere he knew he'd get the view he'd need.

Farmer sighed, and for the first time in two thousand, nine hundred and ninety-nine days, a tension beneath awareness eased within him. Four-and-some years for the waves he made to reach and pass the next nearest sun. Four-and-some more for its light to reach the earth again.

Alone in the sky shone Alpha Centauri.

The first star twinkled, with or without his tears, ten billion wishes already upon it.

Andrew Leon Hudson is a technical writer by day and is technically a writer by night as well. He's an English-born genre author currently resident in Barcelona, Spain, where he's waiting for the world to end. You can find links to his writing and other things at AndrewLeonHudson. wordpress.com. Anything else you've heard is speculation at best.

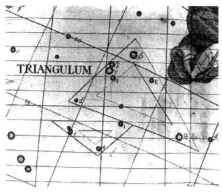

EQUAL IN DARKNESS

ALEXANDRA BALASA

The last rays of sunlight speared between the golden dunes of Ra'Reshet. They struck Kaldune's eyes like javelins thrown by the sun god Himself, reprimanding him for raising his unworthy gaze to the Almighty Light. Kaldune didn't look away as the reverent Cardmasters around him did. He stared straight into the god's fat orange face.

His fists tensed by his sides as the deathly flame winked out of existence in a wash of crimson and magenta. Crimson: a sky painted with the blood of every man, woman, and child who had been sacrificed for the heartless god over the generations.

In the sun's wake, rose Kaldune's master, the god under whose guidance the clouds yielded grateful tears until the sun's hard yoke again reclaimed the land. The moon.

"May He wake with love in His heart," Cardmaster Brasus said, running two fingers down his eyelids in the Resheti tribute to the sunsleep.

A grim smile curled Kaldune's mouth. He inwardly recited the Moonstruck's praise prayer:

We give thanks for the darkness, which lets us be the same
Thanks for veiling color, so the ruthless can be tamed

Thanks for cool caresses, mending sun-baked earth
Thanks for your equality, which gives the worthless, worth

Kaldune ran his fore and middle fingers down his closed eyelids with the rest of the Cardmasters. "May He grace us with His forgiveness," he said, and closed the shutters against the moon's brightening light.

"Well, friends, the fight begins," Brasus said. "Piri, Derris, bolt the doors and summon the soldiers."

Cardmaster Derris raised an eyebrow. "I thought we were only here as a precaution. Surely the raids won't start on the first sunsleep of the year? For the love of light, it won't even get dark out! Our lord will return in a half hour to protect us."

"The sinners are desperate, Master Derris," Brasus said. "They will not wait for the cover of total darkness to try steal our Decks. Not after a summer as harsh as this one."

"Agreed," Kaldune said. Bolted doors would make it harder for the Cardmasters to escape when the time came to execute his plan. "Sinners are dealt bad Decks for a reason. They know they are condemned, and the condemned take great risks."

The Cardmasters exchanged nervous glances. All except Nafari, who leaned against the shutters looking bored as she twisted one of her raven braids around her finger. She caught Kaldune's eye and winked. Heat rushed to his cheeks and he looked away. He cursed himself for breaking character, but the instinct was embedded deeply—merely looking at a female Cardmaster the wrong way normally got his kind flayed.

"They must be unusually stupid," Nafari sneered. "Do the sinners actually believe they can use our Cards, Duras?"

Kaldune forced himself to meet her eyes. "They must know a Deck has little potency in the hands of any but the one for whom it was made, but still—knowing a fat noble had his Strength Card stolen would make a fit street rat that much more likely to attack him in pure daylight."

That was why his fellow Moonstruck had spent last winter orchestrating the losses of the Cardmasters' most advantageous Cards. Fire from Master Derris, who'd once stalked the streets a beacon, incinerating lethargic plantation workers and drowning uprisings in flames. Growth from Master Veru, whose fields had since become as arid and barren as any poor farmer's. Mass starvation was unpleasant, but it was necessary if the people were to grow desperate enough to revolt.

The most instrumental loss, though, was Brasus's: Love. Without his Love Card, he was just a fat man spouting praise to a god who hated His children. The people had stopped attending Brasus's religious services, stopped paying homage to his angry god, stopped massacring their own in ineffectual sacrifices. High Priest Brasus called himself the intermediary between the people and the sun. When the people stopped loving Brasus, they stopped loving the sun.

And now that summer was nearly over, now that the coming months would be spent in perpetual darkness, they wouldn't need to fear the sun either.

"My fortress can shelter us all this winter," Brasus said. "By summer's end I'll be finished fortifying it and training my personal guard. But... the loss of Master Veru's Growth has put us in a predicament: I'm afraid our stockpile won't last the winter. Going outdoors will, I fear, be unavoidable."

"We should put our Cards in your vaults," Derris said. "If we are to be attacked, we cannot risk having them on us."

The Cardmasters dug into their pockets. Derris, Sutt, and Piri handed over Red Decks, Veru and Utara gave their Green Decks, and Nafari slapped her Blue Deck onto Brasus's outstretched palm with a curled lip. Nafari would get in trouble for her audacity, Kaldune had always thought, one day when the Cardmasters' patience for her 'infirm mind' finally wore thin. But Brasus only gave her a withering look and added his own Blue Deck to the pile in his right hand.

Then everybody turned to Kaldune.

"Master Duras?" Brasus said.

Kaldune inclined his head, his shoulders tensing. "Forgive me, High Priest, but I am perfectly capable of guarding my own—"

"Yes, man, I know your headstrong ways. But you're still new to Ra'Reshet—you've never spent a winter here. The sinners in this land aren't like the ones you're accustomed to in your countryside. They spend the summers building themselves physically, training to defeat us in the winters when we don't have our powers. You are protective of your Cards, I understand, but they are better off in the vault."

"I'll take my chances."

"Some Blues rely on their Cards more heavily than others, High Priest," Nafari said. "Duras is a charming man by nature. Charming men don't find themselves under attack when their Love, Friendship, and Trust Cards are stolen."

A vein in Master Brasus's temple pulsed. That was the best and worst part of getting Brasus's Love Card stolen: freeing Nafari from his clutches. *Best* because she'd taken a liking to him after she'd been relieved from the love spell binding her to a fat priest twenty years her senior. *Worst* because that liking seriously threatened his disguise. Last time they'd been alone, he'd had to hold her at bay to keep her from smearing his elaborate makeup.

Kaldune kept his tone level, cold. "You have a High Priest of the Almighty Order of Light before you, Nafari. Show some respect."

He shriveled inside when he saw anger behind Nafari's eyes. It was always painful, being sharp with her, though Kaldune practiced it often. He'd hoped it would harden him against what he'd have to do tonight. It hadn't.

Killing her will hurt, and you will take the pain. You will take it as you did the beatings at the Compound. Take it, to obliterate magic. To bring equality.

Hisses sounded, scimitars and scythes being unsheathed. Hands flew into pockets out of instinct, but of course Brasus held everyone's Cards, and they were useless without sunlight to power them, anyways. Cursing, Master Brasus hurried into the vault room.

Soldiers' grunts came next, and the raw battle cries of peasants who'd been subjugated by magic for three sun-drenched months. Kaldune felt a pang of sorrow. *I will free them. I will spread the moon's light, the light of equality. In darkness we are the same, and I will plunge the Cardmasters into darkness.*

If his plan worked, this would be the last generation of magic in Ra'Reshet. With all the Cardmasters gone, new Cards could never be made, never pass into the hands of the next generation.

The door jostled on its hinges as a soldier or sinner crashed into it. Every window was secured with bronze bars and padlocked wooden shutters, but sand-clouds from the outdoor fight still sieved through the cracks.

"They're slaughtering our soldiers," Derris whispered, taking Kaldune's arm. He tensed—these people all knew he hated being touched—but luckily he was wearing long sleeves. "When the lord returns we must teach these animals a lesson, Duras, a real lesson."

"Violence isn't the way. We just need to calm the masses," Brasus said, returning from the vault room.

"No, we need to cow them," Nafari said. "Which your cards cannot do. You forget, High Priest, that Love, Friendship, Empathy, and Trust are secondary emotions—privileges the starving cannot afford."

She was right. By arranging to have Veru's Growth Card stolen, Kaldune had assured that this summer the sinners had been driven to the brink. The pain in their bellies and their grief over loved ones' deaths had rendered Brasus's positive-emotion Cards useless even in sunlight. There was simply nothing positive in their hearts to manipulate. Primary emotions now governed the sinners. Emotions Nafari controlled, like anger and hatred, and those Kaldune pretended to control, like fear.

A powerful blow shook the door, making Derris jump. "Are they never going to get tired?" she snapped. "The moment the sun hits the horizon, they'd better sprout wings and fly back to their hovels if they hope to survive."

The sinners always managed to scatter before sunrise, and as a frequent night-walker himself, Kaldune knew they wore hoods and masks during raids to keep the nobility from targeting their families at first sunlight. But of course he couldn't say that. "Let us lead a prayer in the basement," he suggested. "After you, High Priest."

Brasus nodded and left the room, the others filing out after him. Only Nafari remained with Kaldune in the entrance chamber. She wasn't panicking, wasn't cringing at the crashes against the door. Perhaps it was her madness, but she calmly watched dust clouds swirling as their fortress took more blows. The chains along the door stretched and slithered like the building was a living, breathing thing.

Kaldune glanced at Nafari. Something squirmed inside him at the thought of never again seeing the glint in her eyes, hearing that laugh that got on the other Cardmasters' nerves....

She can't be the exception. All Cardmasters must be neutralized. No discrimination—only equality.

Nafari crossed the chamber with a bounce in her step, blue beads rattling in her hair, and wrapped her arms around his neck. "Alone at last," she sighed. Kaldune jerked, his heart popping into his throat. After years of living in disguise, he still couldn't overcome that instinct that told him every move someone made toward him was to physically harm him.

She grinned at his jumpiness, though Kaldune had made Cardmaster Duras's "fear of physical proximity" clear from the beginning. "Really, Duras, I've never had to work so hard to win a man in all my life," she laughed, and leaned forward to kiss him.

Kaldune held her back by the shoulders, playing the scandalized Cardmaster. "Nafari, we're under attack! This is hardly the time, and... why aren't you afraid?"

"Why aren't you?"

He frowned. "You should go downstairs. The sinners aren't letting up—"

"What's your *real* name, Lunatic?"

For a moment Kaldune's brain just hummed like a struck gong. Nafari reached up and brushed the bronzer from his cheek with her thumb, revealing the snowy skin beneath. Her forehead grooved with concentration as she studied him. "It's a decent disguise. Bronzer... is that kohl for the eyebrows and eyelashes? The wig is superb. But honestly, for how long did you think that 'I hate being touched' thing would keep you from getting your makeup wiped off?"

Something snapped within Kaldune, and his old primal response to threats kicked in. Clamping one hand around Nafari's neck, he pushed her against the wall as the other hand whipped out the dirk tucked into his belt.

"How long have you known? Whom did you tell?"

Nafari grimaced, but her lips twitched into a smile. Then she started laughing. "Years and years," she gasped through her laughter. "That's why it's so funny."

"We met this summer. Stop playing with me." Kaldune angled the dirk against her jugular, setting his jaw to keep it from trembling.

Nafari twitched her neck away from the blade and traced his cheekbone with a quivering fingertip. "My poor, deceived Lunatic. What did they tell you at the Compound? That you're worse even than the sinners pounding at our door? They are granted weak Decks, but you... you're so sinful you were denied a Deck altogether? Is that it?"

Kaldune felt his sweaty grip slacken around the dirk's hilt. Outside, the sinners beat at the windows in time with his crashing heartbeat.

And he remembered himself, ten years old, running away from the Compound for the Moonstruck to beg that a Deck be made for him. He'd beat against the Cardmasters' Temple door like these frenzied sinners tonight. Thirty years later, he could still see the disgust that had twisted Cardmaster Brasus's face when he'd opened the door. He hadn't screamed and fled like the others, though. He'd bent to look Kaldune directly in the eyes and said,

"Do you know why we grow old, boy? Do you know why, after decades of life, our hair grows white, the color leeches from our skin and eyes, wrinkles taint our brows and our bodies begin to break down?"

"No, sir," Kaldune had answered.

"Color is holy. We draw our powers from the Holy Trinity of Light. Red is energy: light, heat, fire, motion. Green is earth: life, growth, healing. Blue, my color, is spirit: happiness, love, anger. These three colors of light in combination can make every other on this earth, and this light is granted to us by our lord, the sun. But the more light we use, the more of our life force is spent, the more color is taken from us. Old age, boy, is the powerless, sinful state of someone who has used up their Cards and been stripped of color, stripped of light."

"What does this have to do with me, sir?" the boy Kaldune had naively asked.

Brasus took a strand of Kaldune's snowy hair between his fingers, and with a sinking feeling Kaldune had begun to understand. *"You were born stripped of color. Your hair is whiter than the oldest man's, your skin lighter than parchment. Your skin and eyes burn in the sunlight. This is your sinfulness. I cannot grant you a color and a Deck because you have no inner light, no color with which to power any Cards."*

"My eyes are blue, though," Kaldune had tried, desperate. *"Make me a Blue. I don't care if my Cards are weak like the sinners'. I just don't want to be Moonstruck."*

Brasus shook his head. *"It's creatures like you that have angered our lord the sun. That anger enlarged Him, turned him red, and forced life to the poles of our planet. I cannot grant you a Deck, boy. Be thankful I am granting you your life."*

Kaldune blinked the memory away. Nafari was still before him, chest heaving as she struggled for breath.

"Release me," she gasped, "and I'll tell you everything."

Kaldune uncurled his fingers from around her throat and tilted the blade up. "You're not a Cardmaster. You're a rebel, like me?"

She massaged her neck. "Oh, I'm a Cardmaster, all right. I can't even imagine how your people got you into our circle, how they convinced the others you had a Deck. But you're right: I'm a rebel, too."

The door's thrashing faded to ambient noise as blood thrummed in Kaldune's ears. Maybe Nafari could be saved. Surely he wouldn't have to kill her if she was working against the Almighty Light?

"Don't look so surprised. Did you think Brasus used Love against me because he wanted an obnoxious, half-mad wife?" She cocked an eyebrow. "Have you ever heard of Cardmaster Zayn?"

The oldest Cardmaster in ten generations. She must have been over one hundred when she died. "What of her?"

"She'd grown so old that her hair and skin had become almost as white as a Lunatic's. When she refused to go to the Compound, she was executed." Nafari's lips tightened into a line. "She was my great-grandmother."

Kaldune could easily deduce the rest. Having a vengeful Cardmaster on his hands—and one whose speciality was anger, no less—Brasus had neutralized her in the only way he could: with Love. When Kaldune's rebels stole Love, they'd unleashed Nafari's dormant wrath.

Slowly, Kaldune sheathed his dirk. "What did you mean when you said you'd known me for years?"

"Every summer morning, we Cardmasters look up at the sun. Once or twice in our lives, after we look away, the splotches that we see form distinct names or faces. This is how the sun chooses his next Cardmasters. I first saw your face ten years ago. I've seen it every morning since."

A chunk of limestone crumbled from the ceiling, showering them with dust. Kaldune felt a shiver pass through him.

Nafari fiddled with the beaded braids in her hair. "When I told Brasus and the others, they said it was normal. They all saw people like you in the sun. People affected by the Lunacy. Flukes, they said. The sun hates the Moonstruck, after all. They told me to ignore it. Then I realized they were making their friends the new Cardmasters, regardless of the sun's orders."

"Why would the sun choose me?" Kaldune ripped the wig from his head to reveal closely cropped white hair. "I have no inner light. I'm a sun-damned monster!"

Nafari didn't recoil, didn't even flinch. She took his hand and pressed three rectangular, wax-sealed Cards into his palm. Kaldune shuffled through them—a Red, Green, and Blue. He looked back to her with narrowed eyes. "What is this?"

Nafari moved toward the door, a smile playing on her lips, and in a single fluid motion she lifted the latch.

"No!" Kaldune lunged forward, but it was too late. The door crashed open. A wave of dirty, sweaty bodies poured in, waving sickles and hoes. He halted face-to-face with the muscled man leading them. The man's eyes widened, two pale moons against his sun-weathered skin. He gasped as he took in Kaldune's white hair. The mob huddled behind their leader, paralyzed by the sight of a sun-damned Lunatic clad in holy Cardmaster robes.

And off to the side, Nafari watched, hunger burning in her eyes.

Then the leader screamed, *"Moonstruck!* Kill it!"

The current washed over him. A flash of white. Kaldune woke on the stone floor, hotness spreading from the back of his head. Hands grappled his robes, heels ground into his abdomen until he tasted blood, prongs and sickles jabbed him. He tried to scream, but without air in his lungs he could only retch.

Kaldune curled into a ball, hands thrown over his head, and waited. Like after every failed escape attempt, when the jailors dragged him back to the Compound to beat the evil out of him, he waited. Waited to die, waited for them to stop—it didn't matter.

Nafari's screams cut through the haze of pain. The sinners had gotten her, too. "Fight, Lunatic! Look into the light!"

Between kicking legs, Kaldune caught a glimpse of the sky through the open doorway. A pink strip lined the horizon, the first starburst of sunlight blinking like an opening eye over the dunes. Light infused into his pores and warmth spread from the fingertips of his right hand, in which he still clutched the Cards Nafari had given him. It flowed up his body, extinguishing the agony. Green Health pumped through his veins until gashes sucked closed. Bruises became milky white through the tears in his robes. The sinners paused, weapons suspended and mouths agape.

Then, somewhere deep within him, the warmth congealed into rage. A scream wrenched free from Kaldune's throat. Fire blossomed from his fingertips, bowling the sinners over. Shrieks filled the air as those closest to him burst into flames and fell, writhing, to the floor. Others tripped over them in their panic to escape the fortress.

Light spurred Kaldune on. He climbed to his feet, drinking it in from the tap at his right hand. It fueled him with rage and left him lightheaded. "I was doing this for you!" he roared. Fire sprouted from his hands, wound around the fortress walls. "I was destroying the Cardmasters for us, so there'd be no more magic. So we'd all be equal!"

Nafari used the windowsill to climb to her feet. She limped over to Kaldune, cradling what looked like a broken arm. "The only thing that makes humans equal," she hissed in his ear, "is that whoever has power, uses it."

Fire chased the sinners from the fortress. Fear from Kaldune's Blue Card beat against their backs in palpable waves, making them claw one another in their haste to escape. Green worked in tandem with the others, protecting him, Nafari, and the fortress walls from the conflagration.

A corner of Kaldune's mind wanted to let them go, but the light filled him and he knew he was better than them, stronger than them, that he'd have to teach them a lesson. They'd hated him for being colorless. They'd treated him like the Cardmasters treated them. Now he'd use all three colors of the Holy Trinity to make them pay.

No!

Kaldune forced himself to lower his hand. The Cards slipped from his numbed fingers and he slumped against the basement door, shaking.

Nafari laughed at the masked forms flailing in the sand outside, smoke and a reek like burnt pork wafting from their blackened bodies. Kaldune gazed at her in horror, the residual power still tingling in his fingertips. "What have you done to me?"

"That's what the colorless are: not beings stripped of light, but filled with it." Blood streamed from Nafari's nose and a gash ran like a bloody trench through her brow, but she barely seemed to notice. "White light holds all the colors, Lunatic. You, my grandmother—people like you can use Red, Green, and Blue Decks. This is why the Cardmasters fear you, why they lock you in compounds and call you sinful, why they refuse to make Cards for you. Your power is unlimited."

Head spinning, Kaldune could only blink at Nafari. Her eyes reflected the scattered firelight. "Execute your plan. Kill them. I have already made you the ultimate Deck, one holding all colors of the Holy Trinity. We'll free everyone at the Compound, and together we will rule Ra'Reshet."

Kaldune withdrew the canister of poison gas tucked inside his robes, turning it over in his hands. "My goal was to obliterate all magic, Nafari, to make all men and women equal."

She wrenched the basement door open and gestured into its depths, from which the Cardmasters' whimpers sounded. "Avenge your people, avenge my grandmother."

Kaldune looked at the smoldering bodies in the sand—more of the sun's sacrifices. Disfavored unfortunates, like him. No: people who would still wield power against the weak if they had the opportunity. Like him.

Which was exactly why power had to be eliminated.

Kaldune took Nafari into his arms, pressing her into an embrace. "Thank you for not hating what I am," he whispered into her hair. "But I hate what you want me to be."

He barely felt her body tense before he pushed her backwards into the basement. Kaldune unscrewed the canister's lid and tossed the hissing thing after her. He locked the door.

A chorus of screams sounded from below, but the emptiness within Kaldune kept him from feeling them even as tears blurred his vision. He flipped his hood up and stepped over charred bodies into the rising sun. A tiny sickle-shaped moon still graced the sky. Kaldune recited the Moonstruck's praise prayer, because he didn't want to be inferior or superior. He wanted to be equal.

And, in darkness, he was.

Alexandra Balasa is a PhD student, TA, writer, and magazine editor at the University of Texas at Dallas. Her greatest achievement is playing Magic: The Gathering with Brandon Sanderson one time. Although she ponders existentialism, adores owls, and collects rocks, she promises she is not a cliché. She is a little obsessed with dismantling binaries, though she rants about Derrida far more than she actually reads his work. Her writing has appeared in venues such as PodCastle, Cosmic Roots and Eldritch Shores, and Deep Magic. You can follow her on Twitter at @BalasaAl.

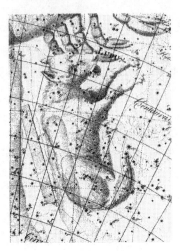

BETTING ON STARLIGHT

ISAAC E. PAYNE

The *Sun-Chaser* casino was closed tonight, but all one thousand of its winking lights still mocked the stars. The logo, a shimmering wolf pursuing the sun, was backlit with golden bulbs.

As she walked toward the hum of incandescence, June Breetle noted that she could not glimpse the stars. An aura of light shrouded the city sky; only Sirius shone through. And airplanes.

Taking a deep breath, June straightened her lapels, dusted with patterns of Orion and Scorpio and Ursa Major. She pushed through the revolving door.

When Jonathan Olasson, the casino owner—and illumination dilettante—had come up to her after her failed light pollution proposal at city hall, she had not expected him to be so polite. He was intrigued, he'd said, by her conviction that streetlamps and porch lights and rattling incandescents were causing humanity harm.

That's when she saw the gleam in his dark eyes. It looked like hunger to her. He offered her a deal, the chance to make change happen outside the boundaries of the city's back-and-forth tomfoolery.

She brushed past the craps machines and the slots, wove around the wheels and felted tables. Every possible bulb was flashing or fading in and out—red, green, a startling white. The air was cool and tasted of plastic and cheap liquor.

The blinking lights made June squint—they were the very kind she'd condemned in her video essay for causing headaches and fatigue. This place was everything June disliked. Perhaps she should have stayed home, penned another light reduction plan. But she was tired of writing proposals that would never come to fruition.

"Ah! Ms. Breetle, glad you could make it. We almost started without you." Olasson straightened the sleeves of his pitch-black blazer.

He sat at a half-moon table, green-felt-lined, with stacks of poker chips and crystal whiskey glasses. Two other men were already seated there.

"Fashionably late," June said, pulling up a seat. The overhead lights buzzed ever-so-slightly. Just enough to be irritating. She studied the others and realized she knew them from the front page, from Forbes magazine, and from ads on television.

The man directly across from her scratched his graying mustache. "Anyone late to a poker game is at a disadvantage, Ms. Breetle."

"How so, Mr. Channingsworth?" June clasped her hands in her lap to stop herself from fidgeting with her jacket buttons.

"I often say that the most important moments are right before the game," Channingsworth said. She knew his type: endlessly a thinker, but always a shallow one. "It's when you get to know your opponents, when you see their tells... and their *faults*."

June smiled as best she could. "I already know all I need to know about you, Mr. Channingsworth. About all of you." These men were the kind who walked every waking moment beneath the gleam of electricity; they drank light straight from the bulb, and the only darkness they ever saw was the microsecond blink of an eye. They were moguls of cheap, harsh light.

"We can say the same of you, Ms. Beetle." That was Clancy Dytalov, the largest man at the table, both in size and reputation. He alone was responsible for millions, if not billions, of lights across the state, the

CEO of Dytalov Industrial Power. "Your video was quite…inspiring."

Jonathan Olasson grinned wolfishly. "Tell me, Ms. Beetle, what spurred you to such hatred of our interests in… illumination?"

June counted off the shards of luminance in the man's eyes. "I don't hate light, Mr. Olasson, no matter what people say."

The men exchanged tolerating glances, the kind that June was used to receiving at city council meetings and from profit-hungry business owners. They had no respect for a woman of science, even if the facts were all in her pocket.

"Let me ask you this, gentlemen," June laced her fingers over the felt table. "What about light intrigues you? Why is every casino, every hotel, every train station you own ablaze with sodium bulbs?"

The good humor drained from the room.

"People fear the dark, Ms. Breetle," Dytalov said, fingering his spotless belt buckle. "It represents the unknown. When people don't understand a thing, they tend to hate it."

"Light is good for business," Channingsworth added, "Creating a comforting, bright, environment keeps people coming back. It's science."

June forced a smile. Channingsworth thought anything—stacking poker chips, drinking whiskey—was a science if it worked for him. He liked to keep "science" in his favor.

"Science," June countered, "also shows that too much light—the wrong kind of light—adversely affects biorhythms in humans and animals. Not to mention what it does to our skies."

Dytalov held up his beefy hands, palms out. "Alright, Ms. Breetle, we know your stance. Let us get to the real reason we're all here, shall we? A friendly game of stakes ought to solve our disputes."

Channingsworth downed his whiskey in a single gulp and sat straight up in his chair. Olasson didn't move.

"Let's," June said. She felt a single bead of sweat slide down her back.

The dealer shuffled the cards with uncanny speed. They were new, straight out of the cellophane—backs smooth and shiny. "The stakes,

Mr. Olasson?" he said. His voice was an oil slick.

Olasson fingered wolf-headed cufflinks and said, "I want to give you a chance to make a change, Ms. Breetle. Because your dedication to this so-called 'light pollution' moves me."

June seethed, but held her tongue. "Go on."

The casino owner smirked, picking out one of each kind of chip and placing them on the felt. "The bets are, at a microlevel, representative. For instance, this white chip, the lowest value, is worth a single star. And this black chip, the highest value, is, say...." Here Olasson ran a finger around the edge of a chip. "A galaxy?" He paused to give her a meaningful glance. "A nebula?"

June raised a brow.

"In the end, Ms. Breetle, you can turn your chips in for something more tangible: a casino, a parking lot, a shopping mall. We will still own these places, but they will undergo the changes you see fit. For every chip *we* have at the end, those places are forever out of reach from Ms. Breetle's efforts, no matter what policies come down the line."

Dytalov nodded vigorously. "Yes, yes. I like this idea very much. May the best bets win!"

She knew this was exactly their kind of game, and that they believed they could play it to their advantage. Channingsworth controlled most of the city works, including every streetlamp, every glaring beam on a statue or monument, and Dytalov could snap his fingers and turn off power for miles. They were in this together.

June did not want the responsibility, did not want to have to be the one to fight against such power. She was a teacher, an astronomer—not some science fiction action hero. Star-wielder? That was not her.

But she was here. And she had to do what she could, to convince these men that their light was destructive, or at least try to beat them at their own weird game. Backing out now would just assure them of their own invincibility.

Who knew, maybe she'd awaken that "hold 'em" side of herself that had lain dormant since grad school.

"Deal the cards," June said, taking a sip of her whiskey.

Olasson smiled, teeth blocks of overpowering white. "Excellent."

Dytalov and Olasson slid their blind bets onto the felt. June had to blink to convince herself, but—somehow—the chips were glowing as if they were actually little stars.

Olasson was still smiling his curious smile. Perhaps the chips had LEDs?

June pulled her cards up to look. *Five of spades, three of hearts.*

Channingsworth went in, a smile tugging at his mustache. He noticed June watching him and quickly covered his jaw with his hand, pretending to contemplate.

"Fold," June said, and passed her cards to the dealer.

"Not a good start, Ms. Breetle," Dytalov noted, raising the bet.

June feigned a nonchalant shrug, "It's early yet."

"So, it is," Olasson said. He watched the flop like a predator, eyeing the cards as if they were his and his alone. June would have to stay on high alert.

He ended up winning with a heart-club straight, and stacked the small pot to the side.

There were runic symbols on the chips—had she noticed it before? June could swear they pulsed. She bit her tongue. They couldn't *actually* be starlit, could they? She slid a white chip into her palm, feeling its warmth. It was impossible, but it had a feeling of *expansiveness,* like it was radiating heat from far away.

But that was ridiculous. They were just expensively manufactured chips, meant to enhance gameplay. Or mess with her head. She shook it off, determined not to let them get to her.

The next six rounds went swimmingly. June held on until the end, raising and raising, throwing out a pair of jacks, a satisfactory flush, and more than a few bluffs. The piles of distant stars became towers, the nebula blossoms and spiral galaxies rose skyward, and she was happy with her three-high stack of what she somehow knew were *complete constellations.*

"You have a knack for the bluff, Ms. Breetle," Dytalov said, doling out more whiskey. "Best watch it doesn't catch you."

June didn't want the advice, but she paid more attention after that.

The following round went on for quite some time, with everyone raising and calling, and by the flop, a massive sum had been laid out: June pictured a night sky filled with close, bright stars.

Then Channingsworth folded and Olasson laid his wolfish eyes upon the communal cards—black, red, black, red.

"Very nice," Dytalov chuckled, pushing in the rest of his chips.

Frantically, June counted up her remaining chips. Twice as many as Dytalov, but was she willing to take the risk? At this point, she was set for a full house, but Dytalov's confidence, his smirk, unsettled her.

"Call," she said after a moment. Better to risk it than lose what she'd already put in.

Olasson matched, and they all checked the next way around. The air was supercharged—so much on the line here, for everyone. June tasted the sweat on her top lip. *Gotta make those college days pay off.*

The last card hit the felt like a thunderbolt. Jack of spades. Olasson broke into a bout of shrieking laughter and threw down his hand.

Straight flush of spades. June scrubbed her brow. Maybe she'd been right: she was no "Star-wielder."

Dytalov's confidence melted away as he drained his third glass of whiskey. Three of a kind.

Olasson could not maintain his composure as he pulled in stacks of chips, his features set in sharp relief, as if lit by photography ballasts. In her periphery, she caught a faint *aura* around his body, like shimmery cars in July heat.

But the dealer was passing out cards again.

Almost immediately, Channingsworth went all in, his pitiful pile of chips nothing to Olasson's horde. June peeked at her cards. *Queen of hearts, three of clubs.* She had to play this, or it was Olasson's game.

She called.

The dealer laid out the flop. Something like smoke curled off the cards Olasson clutched. He licked his lips compulsively.

June's grounding in science was firm; she trusted her own logic and reasoning. But something wasn't right here, and she had read enough science fiction to know that whatever it was, it probably wasn't good. Olasson's impossible aura was now plainly visible, his pile of chips grown dull.

And then she knew. He was *consuming* them, sucking at the light as if it was lifeblood. Every chip (every constellation, every star) that came into his hands. Was he some demon feeding on starlight, or an extraterrestrial, lost and trying to survive?

The game continued, and the more June watched Olasson the more she was convinced that, whatever else he was, he was also sick. The pallor of his face, the sweat beading on the backs of his hands. A wildness in his eyes. Light was his lifeblood, but it was also his downfall.

When the next card came around, Olasson raised. His hands trembled as he parsed out exactly as many chips as June had left—her few stars, a galaxy, a moon.

She scratched her brow and out of the corner of her eye she saw Dytalov smile. This made her mouth go dry. He'd watched her, commented on her bluffs, and seen a tell she hadn't known she had.

"Your turn, Ms. Breetle," Dytalov said. He was smug, so much so that she doubted he'd seen Olasson shimmer through his sweat.

She assessed the chips she had, the last ones free from Olasson's greed. Did he have limits to what he could consume? What would happen if he was filled to bursting?

"All in," she said, stroking the white chip she cupped in her hand.

The last card came out—nothing that could save her. Her only hope now was her bluff. In more ways than one.

Channingsworth—what a miserable player, did he understand the mechanics?—folded.

June scratched an itchy eyebrow. "Well, I guess this is where it's all decided." She smiled. Gods, she hoped this worked.

Olasson took a large gulp of his whiskey. June saw beads of the liquid evaporating from his lips. "Your light is mine, Ms. Breetle." He laid out his cards: a straight.

June gave slow consideration to her cards, smirking. Olasson tremored. With a flourish, she tabled them. All three men erupted in mirth. Dytalov clapped Olasson on the back, but he recoiled, his skin blistering and raw. Somehow, he managed to look no worse than *chagrined*.

Olasson's laugh echoed, as if brought from far away, bouncing back and forth through a tunnel of light. His lips curled into a rictus of greed, and his body began to change.

Olasson's nose plunged brutally into a snout. His back arched, and his hands bent and twisted to improbable points. The suit fell away in wisps, wolf-head cufflinks winking at June before rocketing off into the casino. Her mouth dropped open. She hadn't known what to expect, but it hadn't been this.

"Your light has fed me for centuries," Olasson boomed. "Every flicker, every *photon,* comes back to me, Sköll, in the end."

Dytalov and Channingsworth chuckled as the wolf—Sköll? The Norse myth?—reared up at the surrounding lights, the neons, the incandescents, sucking light from them like juice through a straw. For every bulb that winked out, the celestial wolf bristled and grew larger, brighter, until June's disbelief finally hit its melting point and bled away. *This was really happening.*

The two moguls couldn't contain themselves, ran their fingers through Sköll's hoarded treasure, pocketing chips for any dregs of light. So, there'd been real starlight in those chips after all, activated by some sorcery of Sköll's.

The wolf's white-hot hackles raised, spraying mad sparks of light into the darkness. "What is this?" The voice shook the rafters. "Such betrayal... is asking for punishment."

Dytalov trembled, chips falling from his fat fingers. "Y-you said if we threw the game, made Breetle lose her light, we'd get our share!"

June was too shocked to feel more than disgust. Looking at the monster Sköll drained all emotion right out of her.

"Your greed has addled your senses, mortal," Sköll's lips curled, "Only trust a ravenous wolf to be hungry." He launched himself through the air, at the two moguls.

The poker table snapped in two, the felt seared by superheated claws. June and the dealer fell backwards in a spray of cards and chips that now looked dull, ordinary. Dytalov screamed.

The dealer lay still, head resting against the leg of an adjacent table. June crawled out from the debris and checked his pulse.

"You wanted her starlight, not mine!" Channingsworth's voice was a whimper.

Sköll hacked up a laugh, "Your light is brighter than the sun. Sköll will take it all."

June wanted to help. She felt useless, hunched behind the broken table. But her heart fluttered. She'd never felt more ordinary. She was no wolf slayer. She was a teacher and an astronomer. Had she ever known herself better?

Channingsworth moaned as Sköll arched forward, claws digging into his jacket. Instantly, the corduroy began to smolder, and the odor mixed with that of raw electricity in the air.

She wouldn't admit it to just anyone, but June had spent countless afternoons reveling in fantasy scenarios, and here she was, about to watch a man get the life sucked out of him, for real. She trembled. Her stomach filled up with ice, and she *vibrated* with fear.

Sköll beared his hell-lit fangs, their very image enough to burn imprints on Channingsworth's face and make his mustache smoke.

June looked for something, anything, that might hold Sköll back. Beneath the cindered cards and blackened felt, a single flash of light caught her eye. The white chip! June dove for it and palmed it, feeling its warmth immediately. This was not the death heat emanating from Sköll, this was *sunshine warm. Our own sun!*

Channingsworth's screams threatened to shatter all the glass in the building, and the shape of Sköll was so aggressively bright that June had to close her eyes. The chip in her hand pulsed and again she thought of the sun, inviting it into her mind's eye. Her limbs began to calm, like a sunset, her fear ebbing away.

"Wolf!" June rose to her feet as Sköll turned his drifting-light eyes to her. They were aflame for hunger, for more light, for the hard bulbs of streetlamps and the vastness of stars. And she would give it to him. Sun-Chaser. He was the Sun-Chaser, after all.

Sköll dropped Channingsworth, and lunged for her. But June hurled the chip right into the void of his maw and rolled out of the way.

Sköll swallowed. He began to expand, the edges of his being radiated like solar flares. His laugh was the rumble of a black hole, if black holes had sounds.

Gorged on the sun—that last chip pushing him over the edge—the wolf pushed against the ceiling, against the craps machines and the slots. Bulbs melted to globs of glass and filament, and set the carpet ablaze.

The terrible light around his body seared June even as she shielded her face and closed her eyes. Her tongue swelled, her lips chapped, and sweat coated her skin. The pressure dropped, and popped her ears.

Sköll howled heat and fury. "You've turned *Midgard* to a pool of light, and it will feed me for eternity!"

June panted, crawling away from Sköll's expanding heat. She thought of the sun, reaching into him from our own solar system, deep inside his stomach, burning him from the inside.

Sköll's mirth turned foul, he screamed, and windows actually shattered. June could make out Sköll's body through squinted eyes. It was bloated to a terrible size, flickering orange and red.

It collapsed in on itself.

June was thrown blind to the wall by heat and light.

In the moments after, June listened to shards of glass from broken bulbs tinkle as they hit the floor. The place smelled of burnt hair and ozone.

Dytalov was shaking Channingsworth, unwary of his burnt face. The dealer stirred, more glass falling from his clothes.

June climbed to her feet, wobbling a bit, knees unsteady. Globules of glass pebbled her jacket, and her white button-down would never be white again.

Dytalov cursed at his phone. The screen was black. "Someone call an ambulance!"

But June's phone was dead too. Everything seemed dead. It was eerily quiet in the casino. The dealer pulled himself to his feet, rubbed his head.

"Jack!" Dytalov lumbered around the broken table to the dealer, "Help me get him out of here!" Together, they hefted Channingsworth's still-smoking body toward the door.

June followed them, not really knowing what else to do. Dytalov and the dealer pushed through the broken doors. Someone was shouting, but June wasn't paying attention. Her head still echoed from the blast. Thinking muddily, she wondered if Dytalov would sue her for the damage.

She picked up one of Olasson's wolf-headed cufflinks, a little melted, but otherwise intact. The eye, a tiny red jewel, glared at her. She smiled back.

Should she get her own cufflinks now, or a pin for her lapel? "Killer of Sköll," "Wolfbane...?" She'd have to think on it.

June emerged from the *Sun-Chaser* casino to a darkened street. The sidewalk was littered. The rainbow array of scintillating lights had been blasted apart, and even the streetlights had been shattered.

For a moment, she stopped to listen. She was surprised to hear the chatter of people and a patter of feet among the faint sirens, but there was one thing she didn't hear: a single, buzzing light. Sköll's implosion had gone out like an EMP.

She maneuvered around glass into the middle of the street. Cars were stalled out up and down, their headlights blown out. People leaned out of windows or stood stock still on the sidewalk, trying to restart their cellphones.

June looked up.

The sky was a tapestry woven of starlight and the umber of the Milky Way. June's breath caught in her chest. It was so bright, so clear! Her eyes weren't as young as they used to be, but she could see more of the stars than ever before.

June Breetle couldn't take her eyes away, so she didn't notice when a group of people formed around her in the street.

"Amazing," one of them said, jaw hanging slack.

"You know," a middle-aged man said to a curly-haired woman, "I don't think I've ever seen them so clearly. Not even at our country house."

"They're brilliant," was all June could say. She stuck her hands in her pockets and crossed to the other side of the street as people began to point out constellations they knew from school textbooks.

June looked up again, just in time to see the tail of a shooting star curve across the sky and disappear into the distance. The crowd gasped and pointed, some exclaiming at having just missed it.

As people began declaring their wishes, June walked back to her apartment. Starlight was enough for her to find her way among these darkened streets, and she hoped that it was enough for the people staring up at the sky too; hoped that they'd not forget this moment in time, no matter how old or bright their lives became.

Isaac E. Payne is a graduate of the 2017 and 2018 Alpha Science Fiction, Fantasy, and Horror Young Writers Workshop. He has presented his research on speculative narratives at NeMLA and has talked about young adult literature at the 2018 Nebula Awards. His poetry has appeared in Abyss and Apex and he has short fiction forthcoming from DreamForge Magazine. When he's not reading weird things on Wikipedia, he is writing about them or tweeting about them @the_paynanator.

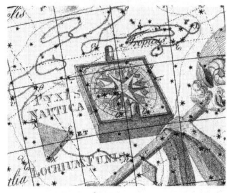

STARS

LIAM HOGAN

They fall from the sky and I must catch them.

I'm stepping off an Indonesian trawler, still tingling from the afterglow, when I feel the distant call. Somewhere in the Northern Hemisphere: Canada, perhaps.

The journey begins by mail van, ferry, and by foot. At the airport, I'm disorientated by the noise and chaos.

"How do I get to Canada?" I ask.

"You'll need to go via Singapore," the girl behind the information desk says. "Where in Canada?"

By now the location of the fall should be on the tip of my tongue. But it isn't.

"I'm sorry," I fluster, "I'm not sure. Anywhere, I guess?"

She looks over my shoulder to a queue of less difficult passengers. "Take a seat," she gestures. "I'm busy right now, but I'll see what I can do."

On the metal bench, I hold my head in callused hands. The departures board shows mainly local destinations: Jakarta, Banda Aceh, Padang. Nothing resonates. My path is murky and confused.

There's a touch on my arm—the girl from the information desk, holding a coffee and something even more welcome: a boarding card. "I shouldn't be doing this, but you looked lost. I've got you on a training flight as far as Frankfurt."

I thank her profusely as she taps her watch. "It's leaving *now,* otherwise I'd love to hear your story. Will you look me up when you come back this way?"

I tell her that if I can, I will, and I mean it, though I'm wary. People misinterpret the warm glow that lingers after a catch, expect more from me than I can give.

Lulled by the rumble of jet engines, I dream of ripening maize, blue-tinged mountains on the horizon. But still no name comes. Have I been complacent? Is this a test of my faith?

In Frankfurt, I thumb a tatty stack of foreign notes, wondering how far they'll get me.

"Welcome back, Mr. Fletcher," the guy working the ticket desk says with an easy smile. It's not my name. It's not even the name on the passport I handed him and can only have been summoned by a computer glitch or data error, but as usual I go with the flow. Mr. Fletcher is a regular traveler between Frankfurt and Calgary and has enough air miles to pay for an economy flight home.

But not the airport taxes. I'm directed to the bureau de change, where my wages from two months on a fishing trawler barely cover the departure fees.

Though I'm on my way, I'm feeling rushed, agitated. As I tuck my canvas bag between my feet, the Canadian across the aisle asks if this is my first flight.

I laugh and say no, and he smiles and says he still gets nervous as well. Tells me he's a farmer and when I ask what he grows, he says maize. Finally I begin to relax.

I sit in the cab of the farmer's pickup trying not to fidget. Ever since he drove away from the airport long stay we've been headed in the wrong direction. Did I read too much into the easy conversation we had as the plane was coming in to land? Should I put my trust in the chance arrangement of airline seats? Intersection after intersection passes us by, each a Doppler shift from hope to disappointment until finally I crack and ask if he's going the right way. He pulls over and, with the indicator ticking, reaches across and pushes the passenger-side door open.

"I'm headed east," he says, "I don't know where you're heading and I thought you didn't either, but you're welcome to find your own path."

The first two cars are Calgary bound and I wave them into the thickening dusk, feeling the time slip away. It's over an hour—an hour of listening to my heart beat too fast—before a truck with a farm feed logo stops. The driver takes in my rough clothes, sturdy boots, and tattered bag and asks: "Looking for work, son?"

I nod, uncertain, and he bangs twice on the panel behind. The tailgate swings down and a brace of strong arms haul me up.

It's dank and dark and the air is thick with tobacco and sweat. My hands twitch and flutter. I can feel the call—insistent, painfully so.

When the truck grinds to a halt, I bolt into the night, laughter echoing as someone calls out: "Don't piss on the corn!"

I plunge through the tall plants, knowing I'm too late. Will I find it lying on the dirt, soiled, damaged, the light bleeding away?

Bursting into the crop circle, I stop, astounded. A girl stands in my place. I feel a tide of resentment, anger, and fear. For a moment, I wonder if I can force from her what is rightfully mine. Then the envy slips easily away as she turns to me with arms spread wide and smiles the smile of a fresh catch and I'm bathed in her glow.

Afterwards, as we lie in the moonlight listening to the wind whisper through the maize, I realize I don't know her name.

"Stella," she says, her naked belly rippling with laughter beneath my head. "That's what my father called me: Stella."

She returns a year later, just as the corn is ready to be harvested again. Dropping off her child—our child—with an impatient wave she tells me she's overdue in Wisconsin. As she steps to the side of the road, a haulage truck pulls up and she gets in without a backwards glance.

I've settled here, doing a bit of this, a bit of that, but raising Oscar, mainly. He's four now and loves to hike. I have to carry him part way, otherwise we'd not get far, but he's always impatient to stomp the trails on his own. I think he likes it best when we set up tent and, as the fire dies down, he can stare into the vastness of the night sky.

Up here, miles from the blaze of the nearest city, far away from the brightly lit ribbons of the roads, away from other campers, away from everyone, the stars are undimmed. The Milky Way carves the heavens in two, an uncounted and uncountable blizzard of frozen diamonds.

I don't feel their pull anymore, but every so often I catch his eyes tracking something he can't possibly see. And then I know that this is borrowed time; that as soon as his legs are strong enough, he'll be off.

Liam Hogan is an Oxford Physics graduate whose award-winning short story, "Ana," appears in Best of British Science Fiction 2016 *(NewCon Press). "The Dance of a Thousand Cuts" appears in* Best of British Fantasy 2018. *He lives and avoids work in London. More details at http://happyendingnotguaranteed.blogspot.co.uk*

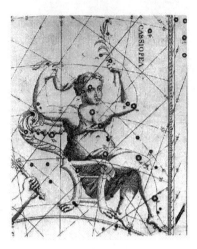

THE VALLEY OF THE STARS

LAURA JANE SWANSON

The Mage stood where the dirt gave way to bare rock. Ahead of him, he could see the cold fire of fallen stars shining on the stone walls of the narrow valley. He could taste them, dry and metallic, on the wind that carried their rough, angry muttering to him. That rough grumble seemed to crawl right through his skin until it reached his bones. Perhaps it was only to be expected, now that they were on the ground, or perhaps they knew how the Queen would use them.

He had searched three years for the hidden valley where the stars landed, and yet he waited. At last, as the sky burned bright in the west and chilled to deep blue in the east, figures appeared, walking single file between the high walls of the valley. The first was a girl, barefoot and bare headed, carrying a silver basket that held a star. She raised it and looked at his face for a moment, but her gaze rested longer on his robes and his amulet and chains, and she said, "The Star Catcher will not talk to you."

He had sought the Star Catcher for three long years, since the Queen had banished her to the hidden valley, and so he waited until the line of Star Carriers had gone on into the forest behind him. Too many children had been taken as Star Carriers, leaving too many villages quiet and empty, but the Queen demanded stars and more stars.

When the last glimmer from the stars in their baskets had vanished among the trees, he conjured his own light, a tiny sphere the green-gold of sunshine through leaves, and he walked into the valley. The sound of his boots echoed against the stone with every step, until the reverberation grew as loud as rain, and then as loud as the ocean, and then as loud as a storm wind. He held his magic-calloused hands over his ears, and still he could not bear it, so he took them off and left them beside the path.

His bare feet only whispered on the cold stone, but his amulets and chains jingled with every movement like a pocketful of coins, and then like an army's worth of mail, and then like the crashing of swords against shields in battle. Their power would be of no use here anyway. He lifted them over his head with clumsy fingers and left them atop a rock, a glinting heap of metal.

Even his robes rustled, first like the turning of pages, but soon like the gnawing of mice and then like the rasp of saws cutting down a forest all at once. At last, he discarded those too and went on in only his leggings and shirt.

The distant stars twinkled overhead and the fallen ones shone in piles in the cracks and crevices of the rocks around him. He wasn't sure how long he walked, shivering in the night wind, his feet growing as numb and clumsy as his hands so that he stumbled over the smallest pebbles, but at last he came to a cave that glowed with the flickering warmth of a fire.

In the end, though, it wasn't the wind that drove him inside. It was that the stars began to fall. At first, they came one or two at a time, streaks of light racing down, brighter and brighter until they burned even through his closed eyelids. As they fell, they screamed. When he could stand it no longer, he retreated into the cave, and there she was, the Star Catcher. She stood with her back to him, silhouetted against the fire.

He had last seen her standing silent at her sister's ascension to the throne. That very day, her name had been taken from her and she had been banished, no longer an apprentice mage at the university in the city. Her hair was longer now, falling loose to her waist, and she stood straighter than she ever had in the city under her sister's cruel gaze. The firelight glowed through her shirt, showing how thin she had gotten, and lit the edges of her face, sharper and tighter than he remembered it.

He must have made some sound, because she looked over her shoulder.

The Queen might have taken her name from her, but he would never be able to see her as only the Star Catcher. "Oh, Anna…" He reached for her, arms open, as though it hadn't been three years since she had left.

She stepped back, hands held up in front of her, and turned away, her hair falling forward to hide her face. Of course she did; she had never been easy with people.

He sat on the ground, not quite close enough to touch her, and waited, counting breaths, until she turned her head a little, just enough for him to see her eyes. They were still blue, but instead of the blue of the morning sky, they were the thin blue of water at twilight. Her face was pale, almost transparent, as though she washed it in starlight. She was more beautiful than he remembered, but it hurt to see her.

One side of her mouth lifted a tiny bit in the saddest smile he had ever seen, and she shook her head.

"I'm not leaving," he said.

He slept that night on the floor of the cave beside the fire, and woke the next morning when he heard her moving around. He poked the fire awake and added wood, and she did nothing to stop him, which he took as some sort of acceptance, though she never came near him. He made tea and set a cup on a rock. She took it after he stepped back.

He followed her out into the watery morning light. The stars on the ground still shone and muttered, but they looked thin and sharp, nothing like as powerful as when they streaked down from the sky.

Looking at them, you would never know what the Queen could do with them—cast lightning upon a battlefield, hear a whisper leagues away, turn a goblet of wine into poison. The old King had used the stars only in dire need, but the Queen used them at whim, and grew more terrible and beautiful every time.

Anna held her hands over them, listening. Their light glowed between and through her fingers and showed all the tiny, tight lines on her face. By the time the Star Carriers came, late in the afternoon, she was moving as stiffly as an old woman. She waited while they set down what they carried, leaving tea and bread and other food, and wood for her fire. Then she lifted the stars she had chosen into their silver baskets.

"Why do you do it?" he asked that night, after the sun had set and the stars were screaming down. "The Queen doesn't deserve this from you." The Queen deserved it from no one, he did not say. He also did not say that the Queen had not deserved his service, though that was also true.

Anna just shook her head.

The next day, he watched her work again. He saw the way she tightened her shoulders before she touched the stars, and the way she let out a silent breath when she set them down and drew back her hands. He saw how pale she was after placing the stars in the baskets, her skin so fine he could see the veins not just at her temples, but also in her eyelids and around her lips.

"Why?" he asked again that night. "You could have been a mage. You would have been the best of us."

She just shook her head again.

On the third morning, she dropped a star. It was small, barely big enough to fill her cupped hands, but it shattered into hundreds of fragments that skittered across the floor of the valley. One struck a pebble and bounced up against his leg. It only touched him for a moment, but it burned like ice and fire at the same time, and it left a white mark on the skin.

She left the stars then and went into the cave. A few minutes later, she returned to kneel by his feet and wrap a bandage around his leg. Her hands were as hot as fire, and her face was as set as when she held the stars. He held out his hand to help her up, but she shook her head and pushed herself to her feet and went back to her work.

That night, after the Star Carriers were gone, he watched her make her way to the cave. Was it just his imagination, or was she moving even more slowly? And was her skin more translucent? As they shared the bread the Star Carriers had brought, he wasn't sure. The firelight was deceptive; it cast its own strange shadows and painted her cheeks rose and gold, brighter than they had ever been, even before the stars had faded her.

When they had finished eating, she sat beside the fire, her hair falling forward, but this time he reached over and lifted it, pushing it back so he could see her face. "Why do you do it?" he demanded. "The Queen is not worthy of this!"

She shrugged, her shoulder blades sharp against her thin shirt.

He grabbed her arm and turned her toward him. "You will die of this!" It came out not as a shout, but as a rough whisper.

She pulled away, but not before he felt the heat of her skin, and not before he saw that his touch hurt her. "So will the Queen."

He understood, then, and that hurt more than the moment when the star fragment had touched him. The Queen was growing as terrible and beautiful as the stars themselves, as though they were burning away everything human about her. If Anna sent her enough stars, the Queen would die. But how could Anna live that long? She was fading more each day, and there was nothing he could do to ease her pain. She was no longer simply uncomfortable having someone near her; contact with the stars had made human touch agony.

The next morning, he watched which stars she chose: small ones, mostly, the blue and white ones that washed all the color from things. By mid-morning, he had seen her set aside a dozen for the Star Carriers. He followed her down the valley to a nook where the stars had collected in a heap. When she began to move some out of the way, he picked one up himself.

It was only a tiny yellow one, but it was heavier than anything that size could possibly be, and it buzzed under his touch so that his very bones ached. It burned like ice and fire, of course, but his hands were half numb from the years of magic, and he moved quickly to drop it to one side.

He turned back to find Anna staring at him in horror. "You can't," she whispered.

He made no answer, except to pick up another star.

By the middle of the afternoon, he could do no more. Even his magic-toughened hands were cracked and raw, and his body ached as though with fever. But when the Star Carriers came, they took more stars than ever before.

When a week had passed, the skin on his hands began to look like Anna's, smooth and pale and faintly silver, all his calluses burned away. By the middle of each day, Anna was pausing to lean against the rocks after each star she touched, and he was choosing more of them than she was.

At the end of another week, Anna was hobbling even when she left the cave in the morning. He walked out of the valley, past his robes and amulet and boots, back to the forest to cut a stick for her to lean on. Her touch left the bark charred and ashy, but it held her upright.

At last, at the end of the third week, Anna could not rise from her bed without help. The few moments to lift her to her feet left her face covered with silver tears that glowed faintly in the shadows. He barely felt the pain of his own star-burned hands.

She crept slowly outside, but she could barely bend to touch the stars. She watched as the Mage sorted them himself, his head down so that she could not see what it cost him to go on working. She chose only one herself, late in the afternoon, a single star of the brightest blue. She trembled as she lifted it, and the Mage had to take it from her before it fell, but she smiled over it. And at last, when the Star Carriers had gone and the sun had sunk below the horizon, she lay down on the floor of the valley. "Thank you," she whispered, and she closed her eyes.

When the stars were sparkling overhead, he lifted her, heedless of the pain. He had thought to bury her in the forest, but he couldn't even carry her as far as the cave before the stars began to fall.

When morning came, he went out into the valley again. He found the new-fallen stars piled where he had left her, shining in heaps among her bones. He began to sort through them, one by one.

The Queen would have her stars, all that he could give her.

Laura Jane Swanson holds a degree in biochemistry and has done graduate work in molecular biology and science education. She lives in Indiana with her family, where she dreams of the coast and knits lots of socks. She writes science fiction and fantasy.

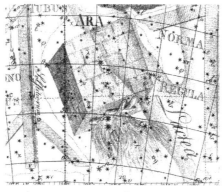

EARTH EPITAPH

R. JEAN MATHIEU

Five thousand years before the end of the Earth, the star called WR-104 went supernova. Over the intervening centuries, its deadly gamma-ray burst hurtled across silent planets and empty space on a death-errand to that distant world. And, in the intervening five thousand years, Earth learned to listen, and learned to see, and learned to contemplate its coming demise.

Mount Pleasant Radio Observatory was far from the chaos of downtown Hobart, and the roads were blocked, but it was only a matter of time.

Campbell shut the door behind her and, for all the good it would do, turned the latch.

"How're things here?"

Robinson glanced at the readout. "Arecibo went offline, and Socorro... and Dominion, in BC."

She turned back to the black Canadian. Campbell's jaw was set. "I'm sorry, luv. Any luck out there?"

Campbell hadn't found anything but a few old teabags. They had no mugs, so she made Lipton's in little Dixie cups, and joined Robinson at the monitors.

"Arecibo..." Campbell breathed. "They fired off the message, right? To the M13 cluster? Big deal in my history books, but...."

"Yes-s-s, I remember." Robinson made a face. "I was just a little girl. I wondered how aliens were supposed to understand what we were saying when I couldn't. And with just a weak radio pulse."

"Not like anyone'd mastered stellar resonance by then." Campbell replied.

"Thanks much for that, luv." Robinson nodded. Her face turned sour. "It wouldn't be hard, now we understand the principles. Could turn the sun into a giant telsat, if we wanted. Light her up so bright you could see it from WR-104. Leave a bloody message!"

Both women settled into their teacups, thoughts stuck on the gamma-ray burst.

Campbell spoke.

"But why stop there? Could trap the signal in the sun's magnetosphere, let it broadcast once each rotation until the sun goes nova."

Robinson glared at her.

"Because Fermi, luv." She turned away, toward the monitors. "Active SETI's fine if you still believe in little green men. But the Great Silence...."

"Don't we have the solution to Fermi's Paradox?"

"Sure. Which of the dozen?" Robinson still looked away.

"Annis' Phase Transition hypothesis. It's only in the last billion years that gamma-ray bursts have been infrequent enough to allow advanced civilization...."

Robinson grunted.

"Charlotte! GRBs're getting less frequent as time goes on. It's silent out there now, but it won't be for long. We're just... early to the party."

Robinson didn't speak, only sipped her tea and turned over Campbell's words. When she turned around, something in her eyes was more maternal than scholarly.

"Fair enough, MacKenzie, fair enough."

Campbell nodded. Robinson finished her tea, and refreshed it. She sat back, listening to the creak among the buzzing and whining.

"Well," she started, "if there's proto-civilizations out there, they might... listen. First thirteen primes, to get their attention, then code a message through polarization modulation... at the very least, they'll know we were here."

Campbell's smile was thin, tired, and warm, like Campbell herself.

"Hóson zêis phaínou..." she sang. "Think I've got just the message in mind."

Robinson's wheels were already turning.

"...have to wait for sunrise, at least. We'll hit Sol ourselves. No relays. We don't know if anybody's even alive to relay to. And for your heliotrans to work, timing's going to have to be perfect."

"Yeah, and we'll need to modify the array some, hook it up to the generator direct for sure...." Campbell bit her lip, a girlish gesture on her seamed face. "One of us is going to have to go out there."

As one, they turned to the window. Out there, Hobart burned, framing the antenna dish array in glowing shadow.

"I'll go." Campbell said, and tried to smile. "Age before beauty."

Robinson opened her mouth, but Campbell waved it off. "It makes sense. Your specialty was signal analysis, I worked with transmitters. You stay here and code the message, I can make the adjustments. And we'll...."

Both women looked into their Dixie cups, into the distant fires.

"...well. We were here."

They finally slept, on empty bellies, around midnight. When Robinson's aching bones let her rise, Campbell was already packed – two water bottles, a radio, and a few hand tools in an old museum tote. She let herself out quietly.

Robinson busied herself with calculations... how much power and at what time and a thousand other factors... and kept the two-way radio humming at her left elbow. Campbell gave regular updates.

"At the array!"

"What was that? Ah. Only a squirrel."

"Power's on!"

"Up in the rafters. I can see Hobart from here...."

Her voice hurt, now. Probably thinking of her grandson in Montreal. Robinson acknowledged, kept working.

"Okay," Robinson said, peering at her monitor, "what message are we coding? Can't be too long... our moment of coronal repeat's in six minutes."

The radio crackled to life after a moment's pause.

"The Song of Seikilos." Campbell said, before swearing. "Sorry, not you. The bolt's stuck."

"The what?"

"Song of Seikilos." Campbell repeated. "Oldest complete musical composition on Earth. Found on a tombstone Seikilos left for his wife, circa 200BCE. Took Greek as an elective at McGill, learned it there. Listen."

She sang, and recited an English translation.

"Fitting epitaph for Earth?"

Robinson looked out toward the array, and actually smiled.

"Fitting enough for MacKenzie Campbell, PhD." She turned on the sound recorder. "One more time, luv. For posterity."

The mike was cheap and the radio, warbly. But it was the most beautiful thing Robinson had ever heard.

"There." She said. "Ready. Just need to push the button in... two minutes, seventeen seconds. How are you doing?"

"All set up here. Going to sign off now. You need to focus. Need to... get the signal out. How long?"

Something was wrong.

"Campbell?"

"How long?!"

Glance at the timer.

"One minute."

Quiet hum, then:

"Too hot out here. Send out the Song of Seikilos. Make my Greek semester count for something."

"MacKenzie, what—"

The radio squealed, so hard Robinson had to kill it. Ten seconds later, back on. But no matter how hard she called, only static hum would answer.

What in the—what had—Had she dropped her radio? No. That wasn't it. Robinson knew it wasn't. Campbell was....

She turned to the monitor. Silently, she counted down the last countdown.

"Go on, MacKenzie." Robinson muttered, before clicking the button. There.

MacKenzie Campbell's last wish.

Charlotte Robinson sat back in her chair, and watched the world end.

After the terrible ghastly noise, an entire biosphere igniting in a paroxysm of cosmic rays, there was a terrible ghastly silence. The Earth fell quiet, never to speak again, except for the soft susurrations of water on rock. But the Sun, once every 28 days, sang into the heavens. An endless verse, repeated over and over, a testament to the first star in the Milky Way to nourish life.

Hóson zêis phaínou
mēdén hólōs sy lypoû
pros olígon estí to zên
to télos ho chrónos apaiteî.

While you live, shine
have no grief at all
life exists only for a short while
and time demands an end.

A franco-californien armed with a wok and a word processor, R. Jean Mathieu has hauled sail, served tea, hung beef, sold cell phones, and even used his own coat as a zip-line sixteen stories above the streets of Hong Kong. He writes every flavor of fiction under a variety of noms de plume. He and his wife, Melissa, keep a good table when not writing side-by-side or chasing trains to the next adventure. You can find Mathieu's work in Ecopunk!, Glass and Gardens: Solarpunk Winters, and Amazon.com.

ACKNOWLEDGMENTS

Diane and I would like to thank everyone who helped put this anthology together.

To the many assistant editors from the Alpha Young Writers Workshop and from the CMU English Department, thanks for all your insightful comments—you each get a gold star.

To Laura Sobolewska, thanks for your diligent proofreading. The next round of peppermint tea and soya cappuccinos is on me!

To Douglas "Pete" Gwilym, managing editor, Father Trundle look-alike, master of facial hair, and also long-time friend and former band-mate/neighbor, thanks for your advice, consultations, and late night/early morning/all day chat sessions.

To Barb Carlson, co-founder of Parsec, for standing behind us, supportive to the end.

To past editor Frank Oreto, thanks for being there for us with your expertise and quick wit, both equally appreciated.

To Karen Yun-Lutz, the (organized) wizard with advertising design. This anthology will attract a wider readership than usual thanks to your stellar flyers, bookmarks, and Dark Skies posters.

Special thanks to *Metro21: Smart Cities Institute—Carnegie Mellon University* and *The Science Fiction and Fantasy Writers of America* for helping us make this happen. We're very grateful.

—Chloe Nightingale & Diane Turnshek, 2019

Staff Bios

Diane Turnshek is an astronomer who's received a Dark Sky Defender award from the International Dark-Sky Association. She has been on the BoD of SFWA and Parsec, and founded the critique group Write or Die, the teen writing workshop Alpha, the Spec-Fic Lecture Series at CMU, and Triangulation. Her students from Alpha and CMU joined the editorial staff of the Dark Skies edition to learn the anthology production process. Now she's using drones to create a high-res night map of Pittsburgh. See her TEDx talk "De-Light the Night" on Youtube!

Chloe Nightingale is slowly renovating her Victorian tenement flat in Scotland. She drinks green tea, does Pilates, and has a lot of kids. A former punk trying her hand at lifestyle blogging, you can find her at champagneanarchist.blogspot.com, @champagneanarchist at minds.com, and on twitter @TheTartanVicar.

Douglas "Pete" Gwilym keeps writing novels in hopes he will someday write the one he loves. Meanwhile, he criss-crosses Pittsburgh on foot, laughs and plays with his family, edits stuff, and records peculiar rock albums ("Favorite Monsters," "Bad Songs," "Bonnie Wipes It All Clean"). This is his fourth and final tour on staff at Triangulation. He is being replaced by a bespectacled spatula with impressive credentials. Any Douglas Gwilyms you find on the Internet are Pete.

Made in the USA
Columbia, SC
28 January 2022

54926226R00119